William Cort

Finding Ridley

PLEASANT GROVE PRESS

ISBN 978-0-9980398-1-7

Published in the United States by Pleasant Grove Press, Port Murray, NJ

For Debbie who told me I should write.

Chapter 1

You never know how things will work out. Rick Gordon didn't see this coming a few years ago. He hadn't met Claire yet, and there was no dog in his life. He was happy then even though he was alone, and after that things were going great until they went bad again. Now, in this moment, crumpled on the floor of a dark closet, holding a shaking and whimpering mini dachshund to his chest, he realized just how far he'd strayed from where he thought he was going.

"Quiet now, Pippa. It's just a vacuum," Rick whispered.

Rick and Pippa had taken up residence in a four-story townhouse on 12th St. between Fifth and Sixth Avenues as "caretakers" for his good friend Ian Stoneleigh. He'd bought it but never physically moved in before continuing on to set up a new home base in Singapore. This was not unusual behavior for Ian. He had earned a lot of money running a small hedge fund with other rich people's money, but lately he had been moving from one business venture to another leaving real estate purchases in his wake like a trail of breadcrumbs.

When Ian asked him to stay for a while Rick couldn't turn it down, since it was a perfect opportunity to save some cash for once. The hour-long commute to and from the Fanwood, NJ house he'd eventually inherited from his uncle had taken a silent toll, and Rick looked forward to the extra sleep and a quick subway ride to work. It was surprisingly easy to rent it out for a year. The family seemed nice, and they promised to go easy on the furniture, so Rick and Pippa were off to the city.

"Carolina, I'm going to bring him out now and hope for the best," he called out from behind the door.

"You can bring him. That silly little boy."

This living situation came with a housekeeper, and, yes, Pippa was a terribly named male dog which wasn't Rick's doing. His ex-girlfriend, and the fancy pet store where she got him, had a pretty good idea Pippa was a girl. The poor guy was a late bloomer, and he was born the same year that Pippa Middleton made a splash at the royal wedding. The name stuck, even after the little wiener's wiener was apparent, and by the time Rick met Claire it was too late to change it.

Carolina was a calming influence on Pippa, and he hated to see her go every week. Rick had originally told Ian he could cancel the housekeeper, since he planned to keep to one bedroom and bathroom and take care of the cleaning himself. Ian had engaged her before he left because he wanted it to be ready whenever he decided to come back, so Rick had to get used to the weekly visit.

Ian had told him, "Let her do everything. Act like you're in a hotel."

This didn't sit well with Rick. It felt lazy, and he didn't like the idea of someone else picking up after him, so he would do the dishes, clean the bathroom, and clear up any clutter before Carolina arrived. She would do the laundry, dust, and vacuum; all of which was a great help until Pippa saw the machine come out of the closet each week. The house had four floors plus a lower level, so it was easy to get the dog out of sight of the vacuum, but it was impossible to erase its taunting hum.

"That vacuum is Pippa's nemesis, Carolina."

"I know. Poor Pippa," she said as she knelt down. "He's such a cute little boy."

Pippa rolled onto his back as she rubbed his belly softly.

"Thanks, Carolina. I think he may be in love with you. We'll probably be seeing you next Monday."

"You're working from home now?"

"No, I'm off on Mondays now, and I sense the job is coming to an end. I might take Pippa somewhere for a long weekend. The problem is now I don't have a place to go."

Carolina gestured around the room and said, "What's wrong with this place?"

"I should be happy here, right?"

"I would say so, yes," she said with a glint in her eye as he smiled at her.

He was attracted to her, and she could tell. They'd had some laughs during her last two visits, and sometimes she'd reach out and grab Rick's arm when something particularly amused her. It felt very natural, but she was newly divorced, and Rick didn't want to force anything. He also wasn't ready to fall for someone again, but that didn't matter because she didn't think of him that way.

Carolina winked at Rick, patted Pippa on the belly one more time, and walked down the stairs with her bag slung over her shoulder. There was a funny squeak in the middle of the first flight. Rick loved the sound and realized it was probably the last time he'd hear someone else on the staircase until she came back next week. Pippa looked at Rick and then toward the door and curled up at the top step.

"We need someone like Carolina in our lives, don't we, Pip?"

Pippa gave Rick a side-eyed look and went back to staring toward the front door.

"OK. Let's go for a walk."

The dog began to have what some would consider a fit. He half leaped and then backed away, doing a little evasive dance that Rick could never figure out because it was always different.

"C'mon, buddy! We can't go until you settle down."

Pippa flipped over onto his back with his legs spread out stiffly making it almost impossible to put on the harness. He laid in a prone position panting and looking up at Rick expectantly. Once snared and secured, he began to let out excited, staccato squeaks. Pulling them all the way down the flight of stairs, quickly past the squeak, and into the vestibule, he jumped against the front door, barking with more throat once outside, and pulled hard down the stoop. Then, as soon as his paws touched the sidewalk, Pippa's mood changed suddenly, and he sat down stiffly.

"You know you want to go for a walk," Rick said gently as he always did because this had become an everyday occurrence.

Pippa looked up at him wide-eyed. His nose tip bent back and forth, left to right, slightly up and down. His eyes were fixed, and his haunches were dug in against the sidewalk. The harness, which was actually a coat that made him look a little bit like a cartoon detective, was strained at the hook practically pulling the collar up over his ears. It was a jaunty but sad look.

Pippa walked a few feet toward Sixth Ave. and stopped. They turned toward Fifth, walked a few paces, and he stopped again. He picked him up and carried him halfway up the block. They crossed the street, and he put him down at the corner, finally underway back toward Sixth again.

They hadn't gotten far when Pippa growled and barked at the sight of a woman shuffling their way. She was wearing an oversized black coat and wool cap and was hunched over with her back and neck twisted to one side as she pushed on her cane. She stopped to stand and wait under a small awning pointing at Pippa and laughing loudly over the sound of his frantic barking.

"What kind of dog is that!?"

"He's a miniature, long-haired dachshund," he said holding Pippa back.

She leaned forward, craning her neck dramatically, and Rick started to realize that she was a little bit off. She extended her fingerless-gloved hand toward him and asked, "Is this kind as expensive as one of those Shit-zoos?"

He tightened the leash to slowly pull Pippa away as his barking started to die down, and he made the snap decision to lie.

"I wouldn't know about a cost. He was a rescue, and I got him from a friend of mine. OK, have a nice day," he said as he moved away quickly and waved goodbye.

Claire had paid a lot of money for Pippa. She'd walked into a pet store in Hoboken after a bad breakup hoping the puppies would cheer her up, and there was a very attractive, bearded guy with tattoos wearing a flannel shirt cradling little Pippa in his strong hands. That was Claire's account of the purchase, and he wondered why she didn't just go out with the salesman and skip the puppy. He'd started dating her just before Pippa turned three, and they'd split up by the time he was four.

She said Rick didn't deserve the rollercoaster she'd created out of their relationship. Rick was also "too nice" according to Claire, and there wasn't anything he could do to change her mind. She moved to Colorado for a clean break and didn't want either one of the boys in her life. Rick and Pippa were left to fend for themselves. In a way, Rick hadn't lied to the odd, black-cloaked woman.

"What do you think Pippa? Are you a rescue dog? Doesn't that sound so much better than $1,000 dog?"

Pippa looked up at Rick and jumped against his leg with a stifled bark that ended in a yawn.

"Well, you're priceless to me, little pal. Maybe you were the one who rescued me? I think that's more likely."

They walked on, and he thought about some of the clues he should have seen along the way. Things fell into place a bit too quickly with Claire. It should have been a sign that he had fallen so hard for her and vice versa. She proclaimed herself "crazy," and she was proud of it. She joked that if she became pregnant with his child, she'd throw herself down the stairs. The other tip-off was her unique world view which was, as Rick was now able to joke, that it revolved around her.

He was so full of the first flush of infatuation when they first started dating that he allowed himself to overlook a lot of things including an absolutely disgusting stool made out of an elephant's foot that had a prominent spot in her apartment. Her father, she said, liked to go on safari. She often warned that her family would have Rick sobbing in the corner under the weight of their extreme criticism if she ever brought him home for the holidays. It all sounded fine to Rick. The holiday trip never happened, so no one would ever know how he would have handled himself against the great hunter and the rest of the kin. It was clear now that both he and Pippa had dodged a bullet.

He had shared the relationship events with his best friend Amanda Colville, and she had a hearty laugh when he got to the part about being too nice.

"You're definitely not nice," Amanda said.

"Yes, that's right. I'm not nice," he thought.

He didn't believe it, though. It was, indeed, one of his faults. This niceness hadn't always been channeled toward Amanda, so it was understandable she felt that way. They had become sharper with each other, honed by the shared gains and losses. Their relationship was a cycle of recriminations followed by forgiveness, and they had never made room in between to soften the edge. They had been best friends since freshman year of high school. Her locker was next to his, and the two were so chummy that everyone assumed they were dating. They tried a lot of things for the first time together but never allowed themselves to get close enough to try being more than friends.

The tensions always arose when one or the other was in a relationship. In some ways they probably should have become a couple and been miserable together in lieu of the series of breakups they endured. They would help each other through it but then retreat every time the other found happiness again. It was a sad kind of unrequited love between friends who never wanted anything more from each other, and the shared experience made them stick together. There was neither sympathy or schadenfreude when one or the other became single again. It was more akin to a feeling of loss mixed with jealousy. It was always this strange love, or simply the innate desire to protect each other, that inevitably brought them back together again.

When Claire finally made the decision to leave after vacillating painfully for a week, the first thing Rick did was text Amanda. Claire had left for the airport, and suddenly the apartment was unbearable. She was still everywhere. A combination of lip gloss, perfume, Dentyne, and stale cigarettes hung in the air.

He struggled with the compulsion to put the elephant foot on the pee pad Pippa had been trained to use, but he thought, "What would that prove?" It seemed doubly unfair to the elephant and just another unnecessary desecration.

He knew it was time to get out of there before the sadness and anger started to swallow him up. There was also a feeling of relief and hope, but he had only just begun to sense it through the haze of failure and regret. It always felt like a failure at first, and sometimes it stayed that way. The ones that fell completely to pieces always felt like failure.

Lost in the swirl of bad memories, he had walked a little further than usual with Pippa, and they were already approaching the corner of Waverly Pl. They'd usually turn left on 10th St. and head back to the townhouse. Feeling rain on his face as they turned to walk north, he didn't mind turning in at the corner of 11th St. when Pippa pulled him that way.

"It's funny how much can be overlooked when you fall into a routine," he thought.

A masonry wall with ironwork came into view just beyond the corner building with the French café on the ground level. He'd walked past this spot every day for a month on his way to and from the subway entrance at 8th St. but never turned to look. The wind and rain had died down, and Pippa slowed to sniff the low wall lifting his leg in a show of interest even though his urine supply was exhausted blocks ago.

Peering through the iron bars, he could see old gravestones bolted against the bricks framing the angular enclosure. A gate gave a better view, and a plaque next to it read:

The Second Cemetery of
The Spanish and Portuguese Synagogue
Shearith Israel
In the City of New York
1805-1829

Rick broke his gaze when Pippa suddenly barked and lunged at a large black poodle passing on the sidewalk. He took one last glance at the markers arranged along the wall and on either side of the small brick path, and they started to make their way home.

Cemeteries fascinated him as a child. His mother had taken him to do charcoal rubbings of gravestones on large sheets of paper, and the images of angels and skulls were both frightening and beautiful to him. Some markers had heaved out of their position after more than 200 years, and eight-year-old Rick was delighted to see small signatures and designs meant to be hidden beneath the ground for eternity. They were the marks of apprentice carvers, and he imagined what they had talked about as they chipped away along the bottom of the blank sandstone slab practicing their trade.

The composition of the stone made it a perfect medium for carvers but also left it prone to the forces of nature. The carved face of the rock on some of the stones had sloughed off entirely leaving only a rough surface where 800 seasons of water and wind ground away at the final words. It was Rick's first exposure to death, and one epitaph became engraved in his young mind:

Remember me as you pass by,
As you are now, so once was I,
As I am now, so you must be,
Prepare for death and follow me.

Chapter 2

Pippa was lying across the couch on his back and had settled into his favorite position across the top of Rick's legs at a right angle. He'd eaten, and it wouldn't be long before he was asleep, so he gently eased himself out from under him before he got stuck with a snoring dog on his legs.

"He's so serene when he's sleeping. So peaceful," he thought.

Pippa immediately burrowed under the blanket after he stood up.

He walked into the kitchen and ate a can of sardines while he stared absently at the television in the other room. There were several unopened duty-free bags that appeared after Ian had gotten back from a week of skiing in Gstaad, dropped his luggage, packed again, and left for the airport. A scrawled note on the counter said, "Help yourself, Ricky!"

"What's in here? 18-year-old Cuban rum. Don't mind if I do! A little Caribbean flavor seems like a good selection on a rainy spring night."

Rick poured it straight, sniffed it deeply, and swirled it in the glass before drinking it in one gulp. Pouring another glass, he walked up the stairs into the small sitting area outside the bedroom and stood in front of the bookcase running his finger across some of the spines. He'd never carefully looked at the books before, and the selections were quite eclectic. As he pulled out *Where the Sidewalk Ends* from the middle shelf there was a muffled click punctuated by metallic grinding that sounded like a small circular saw finishing a cut. The bookcase swung out from the wall revealing a room behind it. Ian had made this the highlight of the home tour before he left.

"Dude," he'd said in a whisper, "this is the reason I bought the place. Safe room!"

Rick gestured toward an array of bongs and glass pipes lined along the wall.

"Looks more party room than safe room, but maybe you're on to something? This is what sealed the $15 million deal?"

"Well, I decided it needed to also be a party room, but the previous owner was more prudent. I figure I might as well be prepared to hunker down in here. There's some food and water, booze, and weed. You know, the staples."

Rick pushed the book back into place as he swiveled the door open and stepped into the secret room. "Well," he said yawning softly, "hopefully the home invaders won't be Shel Silverstein fans."

Ian had inherited some office furniture that had either been built inside the room or brought in before the door was installed given the limited clearance when the bookcase turned on its center axis. There was a large, high-backed chair, a small love seat, coffee table, and a desk. He'd also set up his party/safe room with a full media center including an array of four 24-inch monitors he was planning to use for trading. This and the fully stocked basement gym were the only personal touches Ian had time to add before leaving.

He took another sip of his drink and sighed thinking about the gym that beckoned as he picked up a Sherlock-style glass pipe and turned it over in his hand. Ian had left explicit instructions to use the amenities of the house to their fullest, so he felt he was doing the right thing as he poured another shot of rum from the safe-room supply and packed the pipe from one of the small vials Ian kept in the desk drawer.

He wanted to know more about the cemetery on 11th St., and it didn't take long to find the explanation: the small, angular burial ground had once been square and was there before the street.

It should have occurred to Rick given his love of history, but sometimes people can only see things as they are now and not imagine what they once were. The cemetery was the second of three Manhattan locations, and much of it was in the path of progress when the new grid system was put into place. In 1805, this location was far enough uptown to be considered pastoral. It was situated between two old village lanes amidst small farms and businesses. When the street was finally constructed, those who were buried in its path were moved 10 blocks north to the third cemetery that had been positioned safely within the new grid system at 21st St. What was left was the oblique plot with a sharp point protruding in front of the stoop of the building next to it, a remnant of an older time when this side wall made more sense to the eye running parallel to a quiet, country lane.

He pulled up several maps and photos and spread them out across the monitors. There was a photo from 1898 showing three small wood frame houses sitting west of the cemetery. They were attached, and the one at the left next to the cemetery housed A.T. Leitiser Fine Tailor. The house on the corner looked familiar, and then it came back to him. This was the site of the Grapevine Tavern. From the mid 1800s, the two-and-a-half story tavern was a hub of activity and became famous as a place for gossip during the civil war inspiring the expression, "I heard it through the grapevine."

Rick often lost his sense of time with maps. He found a version that was the basis for the grid plan adopted in 1811. The new streets were like merciless fingers scratching through farmland, straight through homes, barns, ponds, hills, and rock. The old lanes and paths that intersected the area would disappear, because they were laid out for the purposes of the people who lived and worked there and not for the greater good of the city that would rise up around them.

He leaned back in the enormous chair surrounded by maps on every monitor and felt his eyes getting heavy. There was an article on the opposition to the grid plan in New York which had been led by the old town's most powerful and prominent citizens such as Clement C. Moore, who is most famous for penning the beloved "Twas the Night Before Christmas." Streets would take years to be constructed, but the plan was the plan, and anything or anyone in the path of progress would be flattened.

Rick was startled by high-pitched yipping on the other side of the bookcase. Pippa had a lot of different barks. This was the "wake up, where are you?" version. It was 2:45 a.m.

"OK, Pip, I'm sorry. Time for bed, little pal. I'm coming."

Chapter 3

The phone was vibrating on the nightstand, but the sound wasn't registering. Even Pippa was still under the covers. It was Saturday, and Rick hadn't set an alarm. Once he stirred or said anything he knew that Pippa would be at his face trying to lick him, so he reached over as gingerly as possible to look at the phone.

Amanda had been texting him. He'd be questioned about that later. "Why did you ignore my texts?!" Amanda was funny. She often didn't get back to people right away, but she expected everyone else to jump to attention whenever she called. They had brunch plans near her apartment on 57th St., so she wanted to know what time he was coming. Pippa was nudging his way up through the sheets.

"I'm already in trouble for missing her text. I might as well have some coffee and wake up before I deal with her, right Pip?"

Pippa nuzzled up against his neck trying to lick his face as he said this and then quickly ran to the staircase barking when he heard his name.

"OK, breakfast time. Let's do it," Rick mumbled following him down to the kitchen.

He thought about the previous week as he filled the dog's bowl. The workload had been unusually light which was a sign that the assignment was winding down. He was about to make coffee and go back upstairs when he remembered he'd promised himself he'd spend less time in the secret room and do something healthy. Pippa was happy for now. He seemed to enjoy a post-breakfast nap before getting on with his day, so Rick quietly made his way down to the gym.

He laughed when he heard the squeak in the middle of the first-floor staircase. It always took him by surprise. It was a cartoonish squeak like a sound effect from an old movie. It sounded almost too squeaky, if there is such a thing. It was a wooden tone that was almost musical.

Ian's gym area was well equipped, and everything looked like a torture device to Rick. It had been set up for cross-training with rings and a climbing rope, weights along the wall, jumping boxes, a pull-up bar, and medicine balls. There were other things laying around in the corners, but Rick wasn't sure what to do with them. Fortunately there was a bike, and that worked for him. It had a screen mounted for on-demand spin classes, but Rick opted to set his own leisurely pace on a brief, scenic ride in the Italian Alps.

Once Pippa had his own morning constitutional down to Washington Square and back, Rick took the F train to 57th St. and walked a block to Amanda's building. Frank, the weekend doorman, saw Rick coming and was waving and chuckling as he came through the revolving door.

"Hello! Hahaha. You didn't bring that little doggie of yours? I have the treats this time!"

"Thanks, Frank. I'll take one home and bring him along next time probably."

Amanda was still in a sweatshirt and sweatpants when Rick arrived at her door.

"Oh, are we going to a fancy brunch today?"

"Don't be smart, Gordo. I'm just about to put on some jeans and a sweater. I'll look presentable for you. Why didn't you wear your tux?"

Amanda liked to chide Rick about his penchant for formal dress. He would usually wear a suit to work even if he didn't have a meeting. He always said, "I never know who I might run into or where I might end up going." For him it was easier to put on a suit rather than figure out how to dress down for work without looking like an aging college student. He hadn't lost any hair yet, and his face was fairly wrinkle free from normal conversation distance as long as he didn't smile too widely. Most people were surprised to hear that Rick was 46, although the age they'd guess had been going up steadily.

They went to a new barbecue place a few blocks away that had a bluegrass band, and the food was predictably delicious and unhealthy. Amanda had the deep-fried french toast, and Rick had chicken and waffles. She was drinking a Bloody Mary with a large slice of bacon sticking out of it, and Rick had a beer. The band started playing one of his favorite songs, "Whiskey Before Breakfast." Rick loved the song for its ambiguity. Singing shortens "before" to "'fore" which makes it sound like whiskey is the entire breakfast. He focused his attention on the lyrics even though Amanda was talking loudly.

Early one day the sun wouldn't shine
I was walking down the street not feeling too fine
I saw two old men with a bottle between 'em
And this was the song that I heard them singing
Lord preserve us and protect us,
We've been drinking whiskey 'fore breakfast
Well I stopped by the steps where they was sitting
And I couldn't believe how drunk they were getting
I said "old men, have you been drinking long?"
They said "just long enough to be singing this song"
Lord preserve us and protect us,
We've been drinking whiskey 'fore breakfast…

Rick was about to mention that it should be Amanda's theme song, but she was in her stride and wasn't paying attention. She was conducting a monologue about Claire and his other exes, prodding like a prosecutor, knowing that he was getting irritated. She was on her second drink, but Rick suspected she'd had one or two before he arrived.

"Listen, I'm fine," Rick said quietly in an effort to set the tone. "What did I do to offend you? What have I done to bring your wrath this morning?"

"Fine," Amanda fired back. "We'll be civil with each other and not talk about the elephant in the room."

Rick had told her about the footstool, so this was another jab at Claire.

"There you go again," Rick mumbled.

"Well, excuse me if I sound too harsh, Gordy, but I've been seeing a pattern with you over the years." Amanda knew these nickname versions of Gordon drove him crazy, and she continued, "What was different about this last one than all of the other ones?"

He stared down at his plate and said, "they're all different."

"I mean what was different with you, El Gordo!?" Amanda was on a roll today.

"I'm supposed to be different with each woman I date, like some chameleon trying to blend in to save my life?"

He was seething with anger suddenly but wasn't sure whether it was because Amanda was purposely pushing his buttons or because he'd pushed them himself.

"This is what I mean, Rick," she said in a maddeningly calm tone. "You know I love you, man, but you screw these things up every time, right?"

"No, that's not really true," Rick interrupted. "First of all, you don't know everything about my real personal life. Only what I tell you."

"Yeah, I can only imagine what a disaster your real life is if you've only been giving me the highlights!"

"Yours is so much better," Rick said under his breath.

Amanda's tight smirk went away, and he could tell she was about to unleash her fury on him.

"Do you really want me to go down the list, and remind you of the failures?"

Rick hated that word especially when it related to matters of love.

"No, it's OK. You might give yourself indigestion," he said hopefully.

"Then let me just provide a brief overview," she said after loudly slurping the remains of her drink through the straw. "Do you remember the girl with the tattoos?"

"Yes, I do. She wasn't really a girlfriend. We were just friends," Rick said as he held up his finger to clarify.

"Noted. However, you had sex with her, and she gave you scabies," Amanda said in her best newscaster voice.

"I'll give you that one," Rick laughed. "That was easily cured."

"Next up: the girl who slipped you a mickey."

"Wait a second," he interrupted, "I'm not sure it was her. In fact, I'm fairly certain it was the bartender."

"OK, Columbo, either way you got drugged and jacked up because of a chick."

That had been the hardest of all breakups for Rick but not for the usual reasons. There was no regret about the girl. Rick and Judy had nothing in common besides their love of drink. She started with whiskey shots at lunchtime and continued after work. She was tall but very slender, and Rick could never figure out how she put away so much liquor without getting visibly drunk.

The last night of their very brief relationship was also the eve of Rick's 40th birthday. He had left work at 6 p.m. and walked to Molly's, a place near Grand Central where they'd had lunch. The bar was packed three deep with commuters who wanted a few drinks in their system before heading home to the suburbs. Rick spotted Judy at the middle of the bar with two young guys chatting her up.

Judy was 28, good looking, and at the bar by herself, so it wasn't a surprising sight. Both guys backed off when Rick worked his way around them and she looked up and reached out for him. He felt more like her guardian than a boyfriend in that moment. Maybe that was the problem. It was more than an age difference. Judy was not for him, and they both knew it.

"Hey, how are you? Happy birthday, almost," she said flatly but with a lilt in her voice to mask her displeasure.

"I'm good. What time did you leave work to get this seat? It's packed."

"Oh, I left at four. Nothing was happening."

Judy's work schedule was loose, and she used her free time getting to know the servers at every restaurant near the office. She was well liked at Molly's, and the bartender placed two beers in front of them as soon as she put down her empty glass despite the throng vying for his attention.

"So, let me ask you something," she said brightly as she grabbed his tie to pull him closer and stared into his eyes. "We've been out a few times now, and you don't make a move or anything. Where is this going?"

"I'm not sure," Rick blurted out slightly shocked that she seemed to be launching into a breakup, and yet they hadn't even kissed. "I like you. I'd like to see where things go."

"So, what are you going to do? Take me home tonight and fuck me?"

He recoiled from her sudden anger but realized she was right.

"I mean, I want a guy who wants me. Wants to kiss me," she continued with a slightly softer tone. "Do everything to me. Know what I mean?"

Rick leaned in and kissed her, and she reeled back and punched him in the chest.

"Not now! I don't want you to kiss me now!"

He was confused and tried to get closer to tell her he was sorry. The bartender came over and asked her if everything was alright, and she just glared at Rick, continuing to hold him by his lapels, which didn't give him the impression that everything was alright.

"Let's have one shot, and then I have to go," she said softening her gaze. "We can talk about this tomorrow. I don't want to screw up your birthday."

He drank the shot of whiskey even though he didn't want it, and they said goodbye at the bar.

He felt a warm flush on his face as he walked west past Grand Central even though it was sleeting. He walked a few more blocks and slipped on an icy curb. Two men helped him up from the gutter, and he hailed a cab to Penn Station. Paying for the cab was the last thing he remembered until he got off the train without his coat or wallet in New Jersey. There were other things that must have happened that night, and he eventually made it home on foot with several cracked ribs.

He woke up the next morning feeling the searing pain in his side as he turned over. The phone was buzzing on the nightstand, and it was Judy.

"Hi, happy birthday. I'm sorry I was so harsh last night."

"That's OK," Rick said. "I definitely didn't have a great night after I left you. Lost my wallet and coat. You don't have to feel bad about what you said. I never thought about it that way, but you're right. I do like you, but I don't think it's going anywhere. Hard to break up when we really weren't dating, right!?"

He winced from the pain every time he took a breath.

"Yeah, wow I'm sorry you lost your wallet. You're a great guy. I think you need someone different though."

Those words rang in Rick's head. Of course she was right. He'd heard it before in other ways, but this was the first time it was so clear. Someone different. That's what Claire joked that he could never be. He could never be her version of tough. He was too nice.

"Hey, Ricky! Where did you go?" Amanda was tapping him on the side of the head with her spoon from across the table.

"Sorry," he said. "I was just thinking about that one. Yeah, we were definitely not a good match."

"That's what I'm saying. You don't choose correctly. You need some help picking perhaps? It's not you. You just need to find someone who actually gets you and someone who you can get, too."

"You're right. Obviously that's what we all need," he said quickly. "Ready to go? Let's take a little walk before you go home."

Rick knew he needed to get her off of this subject because it sounded like she was about to set him up. They crossed the street and walked into Central Park past the horse carriages.

"You know what I really want to do next? I want to write," he said as he gritted his teeth waiting for Amanda to scoff.

"I've always said you should be writing! Just do it." She repeated "do it" over and over while poking him in the shoulder with her finger.

"I know," he said pushing her away. "I need a subject. I can't just sit down and write about former girlfriends or things I overhear in bars."

"Just write about something, Gordie. It can't be that hard."

"I'm not sure yet," he said. "I was thinking perhaps something involving history of some sort."

Amanda rolled her eyes dramatically. "This is your idea of what will sell in today's modern, space-aged world? History? We're going to live on Mars, son!"

She slurred comedically to cover for actual slurring, and Rick didn't think it was very funny.

"I don't really care if it will sell. I just want to do it. Not sure why," he said as he grabbed her hand. "Here, let's go over this way."

"But there's no path here," she complained.

"Occasionally one needs to walk a few steps off of the path to find something interesting, my dear Amanda."

Rick looked back over his shoulder and then to the west. "It should be around here somewhere. There it is!"

He pointed down at the basalt outcropping at their feet, and Amanda stared at him coldly and asked, "There what is?"

"This," Rick said as he pointed at the square iron bolt embedded in the rock. "This is the corner of Sixth and 65th. The southeast corner to be exact."

"There is no Sixth and 65th, dumbass."

"But there was, or there could have been. This bolt was placed by John Randel, the surveyor who started mapping out the new plan of the city around 1809. This was before anyone had conceived of Central Park. He and his team went around placing marble monuments or these iron bolts to mark the position of the new corners. It didn't matter if there was a barn or a farmhouse, or rocky hill, or a road there already. He had to re-survey because his markers would be moved or destroyed. People weren't too thrilled as you might imagine."

Amanda was not thrilled either. "Are you seriously standing here talking to me about this right now? You know I have zero interest in history like most people."

"OK," he said softly. "I just wanted to find it. Let's go."

They walked along the path and out of the park toward Amanda's apartment without talking.

Rick saw history in everything, and Amanda saw only the future and what might be. They were best friends, though, and they loved each other in a way that neither could really understand.

Chapter 4

Pippa was up early and so was Rick after falling asleep in front of the monitors in the secret room. Sunday mornings seemed to be the only time Pippa wasn't riddled with anxiety about his walk, so Rick quickly fed him and they bounded down the stairs together. They turned right and then right again toward Washington Square without incident or pause.

A thin ray of sunlight cut through the fog and touched the corner of the arch. Rick looked up as Pippa stopped to sniff a streetlight. He reached into his jacket pocket to take a photo but realized he didn't bring his phone.

"Moments in time like this," he thought, "they can't really be captured anyway. They're everywhere happening all around us if we just pay attention."

"The Minetta Brook was right here running down the middle of Fifth. What do you think about that, Pippa?"

There was hardly anyone out yet, and Rick didn't really care if someone heard him talking to his dog.

"Right here in the middle of Fifth Avenue." Rick trailed off as he imagined the water of the brook running under his feet.

"Manetta Water," as it was labeled on the Randel map, had an east branch that joined the main stream near the townhouse on 12th St. In the old days it had been prized for trout and its fresh, sparkling water. The original course is traced by the namesake Minetta Lane. Rick loved the idea that it was still hidden just under the surface and perhaps briefly running along its path after heavy rains overwhelmed the sewers.

"People forget that nature beats everything," he thought. "They try to hold it back or change its course, but they can't really win in the end. It's like you can't change history. You can only look at it and say, 'This is what happened, and this is why it happened, and this is how it was after it happened.'"

Pippa was moving right along and even stayed calm when two schnauzers turned the corner at Ninth St. That breed always set him off for some reason, but this morning he just kept going. On the way back they turned down 11th St. and toward the cemetery approaching from the opposite direction of their first visit. He had a clearer picture of the original burial ground's shape and orientation now. The sharply angled walls were originally set squarely between two quiet lanes and extended to the other side of the current street. One of them was Amos St. which ran along the current 10th St. west of Sixth Ave. between Christopher and Charles streets. Even though he'd carefully studied the map it was difficult to stand in the spot and picture it as it was. They walked on, and Pippa pulled him toward home straining at the leash as they turned onto 12th St.

Rick had two messages when they got back. One was from Amanda asking if he was ready for another brunch, which he wasn't, and the other was from his Aunt Mary. The latter was unusual because she hadn't been in touch since Uncle Will died three years ago.

"What is this?" Rick muttered. "I never get this much action when I'm actually carrying my phone. Maybe I should leave it behind more often?"

Aunt Mary wanted to know if he could find some pictures of her mother who was Rick's paternal grandmother. This was not going to be an easy task since Uncle Will had packed a lot of things himself before he became too ill, including all of the family photos, and all of those boxes had ended up in the garage. He figured he might as well begin the search, so he let the renters know he'd be stopping by later that morning. Pippa was already happily napping on the couch after his long walk, and Rick quietly left for Penn Station.

He felt strange riding the train now that he wasn't commuting to and from work. He didn't expect to see anyone he knew, but the door slid open and it was Doug, who was one of the conductors he used to see almost every day. When he saw Rick he thrust his arm out to shake his hand.

"Hey, buddy! Where you been?! Old lady in Hoboken got you on lockdown? Hehe." He was still squeezing and pumping Rick's hand.

"Thankfully, no," Rick laughed as he tried to pull his hand out of Doug's vice grip. "We broke up last year."

"Sorry, man," he said shaking his head as he took off his cap.

"It's OK. It was slightly rough at the end. It's good. I mean I'm good. All is well. I'm living in the city for a little while and renting out my place in Fanwood."

"Oh, OK! I was wondering where you were, and also they changed my job, you know, the schedule, so I haven't been on the same trains. But, hey, it's all good, bro. Same shit, different flies, know what I mean? Right?"

Rick did know what he meant. He had seen a few things on the train over the years. The conductors often got the brunt of people's ill temper, but today it was just a relaxing ride, and the train was pulling into town before he knew it.

The Fanwood station house was built in 1874 by the Central Railroad of New Jersey. The tracks had run to the north of this location for about 40 years prior, but the company had experienced delays getting coal-laden, eastbound freight cars up the slight grade, so they cut a new right of way. Once the tracks were laid the railroad created a real estate company, built a few homes on speculation, and began to lay out a street plan that would wind through the existing farms and woodlands. This curvilinear approach was the antithesis of Manhattan's strict grid that cut so artlessly through everything in its path.

He walked quickly up Russell Road past the old carriage house his Uncle Will had often talked about. This was the last remnant of a farmhouse that had been expanded into a large boarding house called The Homestead.

"I wonder if I'll even be able to find anything in this garage," he thought as he turned to walk up his gravel driveway.

Before moving to Ian's townhouse he had quickly packed what he didn't need and stacked the boxes four high on either side of his car adding them to the ones Uncle Will had put there years before. To his surprise it took just a few minutes to find one near the bottom of the left stack with "Family" written in a shaky hand on the side with ballpoint pen. Uncle Will was habitually disorganized but extremely straightforward in the way he went about it. Rick pulled out a wooden footstool and dragged the box out to the edge of the garage into the light.

"Bingo," he said. "This is it. Looks like everything he would have had."

He sat shuffling through a handful of loose photos holding some of them up for a closer look.

"Here's Uncle Will, Dad, and Mom…"

He trailed off as he looked at their faces. This was his young mother's smile. Rick was a boy when his parents died, and her smile seemed so far away. She told him "it's alright to be sad sometimes, but always remember to be happy most of the time," and he never forgot that when he was feeling down.

"Life is pretty good, Mom," he mumbled under his breath as tears ran down his face. He wiped them away and said, "I wonder what else is here?"

There were a few envelopes and folders under the photo album. The one on top had "Taxes: 1998" neatly printed on it. Rick chuckled, "Well this is the other inevitable thing you don't have to worry about anymore, right Uncle Will?"

An envelope underneath that one had "FOR RICKY" printed in large block letters across the face of it. He stood up and leaned against the trunk of the car turning it around in his hands.

He slid his finger under the flap and pulled out a yellowed newspaper with a sheet of legal paper folded over to mark a page. It was the September 10, 1970 edition of the local paper, and he smiled not knowing what to expect as he carefully opened it to page six. The article at the top of the page bore the innocuous headline, "The Homestead Was Popular Summer Resort," and Uncle Will had scrawled two cryptic notes in the margin: "Why did both secretaries get murdered?" and "What did Weinstein know?"

This wasn't what he'd expected to find. This was a mystery wrapped in a riddle. He turned the paper over in his hand and noticed a Post-it note stuck to the edge and wrapped around the back. His uncle had written neatly in cursive: "Ricky, I know you love a mystery. You should look into this when you have some time."

Will Gordon and his nephew had a love of the unknown in common, and this small note was like an exhortation from the grave; a smile and pat on the shoulder with a push out the door.

"Go PLAY!" Rick heard his own father's voice now as he sat on the edge of the bumper sniffing the faint odor of stale fuel and moldy grass.

"Damn, I forgot to run that mower dry last season," he said out loud trying unsuccessfully to distract himself. "OK, I'm grabbing what I have here and leaving before the neighbors start thinking I'm crazy sitting out here talking to myself."

There was an eastbound train arriving soon, so he walked directly to the station glancing at The Homestead's old carriage house again as he passed.

"I need to see what this is all about."

He sat down on a bench to wait for the train and pulled the yellowed paper out of his bag. Like the headline, the lead was not much of an inducement to read the rest of the piece: "The home of former Mayor and Mrs. Clarence W. Slocum at 75 Martine Avenue North was a popular boarding house and summer resort around the turn of the century. It was run by Miss Emma Boucher and her sister."

"Hmmm," Rick thought, "this is scintillating stuff."

The old boarding house was a "haven for city dwellers, with tennis and croquet courts, and several other conveniences," at one time housing up to 40 people, many of them prominent citizens.

An eccentric and reclusive millionaire boarder named Edward A. Ridley was the main focus of the rest of the piece, and the story was strange. It centered on his love of long, hot baths and his habit of wearing galoshes and two overcoats every day rain or shine.

Rick read further. "Ridley commuted to the city 365 days a year…he always took the 8:18 from Fanwood and arrived back at The Homestead by about 3 o'clock. He maintained a subterranean, cave-like office at 63 Allen St…in the early 30s, he and his secretary Lee Weinstein were found murdered in the office…seven bullets had been pumped into Weinstein's body. Ridley died from 22 blows, mostly about the head, with an instrument believed to have been the heavy, high bookkeeper's stool used by Weinstein."

The article went on to note that the case was particularly baffling to police, since the same gun was believed to have killed Ridley's prior secretary, Herman Moench, two years earlier. Moench had worked for the

Ridley family since he was nine years old. Rick folded up the paper and looked at his uncle's notes in the margins again as the train was pulling into the station.

"What did Weinstein know?"

Chapter 5

Pippa was making his feverish squeaking sound when Rick got back. It had warmed up, so he grabbed the leash and harness, left the detective coat on the hook, and hoped Pippa's emotional momentum would carry through beyond the front stoop.

"Maybe a little change of direction will do us both some good," he said hopefully. "Where should we go now, pal?"

Pippa looked up briefly and went back to sniffing the ground. Turning west on 13th St., Rick imagined the farmhouse and large pond that sat there in the middle of Fifth Ave. before the grid. There was a schnauzer coming toward them, and Rick clicked the button to tighten the leash. Pippa didn't care and was looking across the street instead.

"What's your fascination over there, Pip?"

Pippa looked up at the building again and then continued sniffing the metal grate around the tree.

"That's right," Rick said under his breath, "this would have been the back annex of Macy's when it was on 14th St."

There were washed out red stars within oval plaques on the second and third floors which was the trademark of R.H. Macy. He had been in the merchant marines in the late 1840s and returned home with a tattoo of a red star on his arm. This location preceded the current one uptown at Herald Square as the fashionable shopping district moved northward.

He walked on following Pippa's lead as he sniffed his way slowly along the sidewalk. He thought about the mystery his uncle had just passed along to him posthumously and stared absently at the music students huddled outside talking and smoking in what would have been the store's rear loading area.

Pippa barked once and jumped up against his leg, which was the signal that it was time to be picked up, and Rick carried him the rest of the way home. The dog was now happily curled up on the couch under the blanket, but Rick didn't feel like relaxing. He didn't do well with the in-between stages. It was best for him to be doing something or doing nothing. At that moment he felt like having a beer, so he set off for The Green Door.

Sunday wasn't Rick's usual day to stop in, but Merv was there just the same giving him a wistful look over his shoulder as he stood at the taps.

"What do you say, Merv?"

"I didn't say anything yet, Rick. How are ya?"

"Good, Merv," Rick said as he pulled out the corner stool and moved the stack of newspapers. "Nice to see you on a day of rest for once."

"Not for me. What does this look like to you? I'm not allowed to rest like God or you fancy lads."

Rick had first met Mervyn O'Grady when he worked around the corner on Canal St. He'd grown accustomed to his dry wit and gruff demeanor, and it was always satisfying when he managed to make him smile.

The door swung open letting in a quick rush of light that pierced the comforting gloom. A short man walked in patting his pockets and said, "Hello, Merv! How are you?"

Merv turned around as soon as the door opened and he saw who was coming. He walked toward the back of the bar and faced the television mounted in the corner ignoring the greeting. He stood pointing the remote control at the blank screen like a tableau of a man who desperately wanted to change the channel but was stuck mid-pose. The barroom was empty except for two men at the other end and a woman with a cup of tea reading in the back corner booth. This was nothing like the weekday lunch crowd Rick remembered with crews from neighboring construction sites standing two deep at the bar.

The man shrugged when Merv didn't reply, and he sat down two stools from Rick after slowly removing a heavy coat and cardigan sweater. It was too many layers of clothing for the mild weather, and he was carrying a large manila folder stuffed with papers which Rick thought was slightly odd for a Sunday. He pushed his coat and sweater down onto the stool next to him and grinned as he looked over at Rick. It was a thin smile, and he could see the corners of his squinting eyes flashing behind light-colored sunglasses.

Rick had never seen him before, but the stranger greeted him like an old friend with a hearty, "How are you?!"

"Hello," Rick said as he took a sip and looked at him cautiously. "Sorry, but I don't think we've ever met."

"I'm Fredo," he said enthusiastically and then mumbled under his breath.

"Well, it's nice to meet you, Fredo. I'm Rick."

Fredo opened up his folder on the bar and pulled out a stubby pencil and the racing section from The Daily News.

"See this? See this here?" Fredo was pointing dramatically at the Belmont race results. "This is how you know whether to bet."

Rick had a slight interest in horse racing and no interest in gambling. He figured he already had enough vices that siphoned off of his small and irregular income.

"Ah, that's OK," Rick said cheerfully, "no need to hand over your secrets. Save it for someone who can really use it."

"No, you see here the thing is this. The thing is you can pick the winners. You see?" Fredo pointed all over the page making small pencil marks as he went. "This here. This horse won the last three races. It weakened him. Get it?" Fredo flashed his gaze over Rick's head like a kid in a candy store watching fireworks through the window and kept on talking. "So you bet on this horse that didn't win. Also, if the race is seven furlongs, you gotta always bet the outside…"

Merv put down the remote control without turning on the television and slowly pivoted to face them.

"Hello, Alfredo," he said slowly. "You know only movie stars and assholes wear sunglasses in a bar, and you ain't no movie star."

Rick choked a little trying to swallow his beer and kept his gaze slightly averted. Fredo took off his glasses revealing rheumy eyes with dark red circles. There was a fading, yellow bruise below his right eye. He smiled thinly again, but all of the light that seemed to be shining behind his glasses had gone away.

"OK, OK. I gotcha…" Fredo trailed off. "Budweiser."

Rick was sitting quietly the way he did in the morning when he hoped

Pippa wouldn't realize he was awake. Looking down at his phone he texted Amanda to let her know that the idea of brunch number two had become late afternoon drinks if she was interested. He knew it was likely she'd already moved on to something else but figured it was the thought that counted.

Fredo cleared his throat and said, "Hey, why dontcha ever put the horse races on, Merv?"

Merv flashed his eyes at him and yelled, "Because you keep fuckin' asking!"

He shot the comment back quickly with mock anger as he put down Fredo's bottle of beer, so it seemed that this was not the first time they'd had the exchange.

Rick felt like pressing his luck and said, "What's wrong with the ponies, Merv?"

"Nothin' against horses. Lovely animals. It's just the assholes who have to bet on 'em," he said with a lilt as he went to the corner again and pointed the remote at the blank screen stabbing the air dramatically. He looked over his shoulder and gave Rick a wink and a small smile, which was an expression of great joy for Merv.

"God, I love this place," Rick thought as he finished his beer.

"You'll have another one then," Merv said as he swept Rick's glass away replacing it with a full one before he could say anything.

"Well, alright Merv. I was going to take it easy this afternoon, but…"

"Isn't that what you'll be doin' then? You should take it easy. It's not about the years in your life but the life in your years, right?"

"I guess you're probably right again, Merv."

Fredo had his head down and was making check marks on the racing form. The door opened, and Rick thought the new customer looked familiar.

He looked at Rick and said, "Hey, how are you? Rick, right? I used to see you in here. It's Dan."

"That's right. I don't get back during the week anymore. Good to see you again."

"Yeah, I was gone for a while, too, but now I'm back again," he laughed. "Just checkin' on the job for tomorrow. We got a big installation around the corner for a new sneaker. A whole storefront. Remember when your mother got you whatever sneakers they had in the store that fit?"

"Sure. I think life used to be simpler," Rick said nodding.

"So, what's up with you? Still got that hot girl in Jersey City?"

"It was Hoboken, and no."

"Ah, sorry man," he said as he slapped him on the back.

"No, it's OK. I almost got myself caught up in something bad. She was the worst thing for me and vice versa, but I couldn't accept it. She broke up with me slowly, and I still wanted it to work out."

Rick was telling Dan things he would never share with Amanda. He should have felt comfortable discussing anything with her, but he knew whatever he told her would be dissected and possibly used as ammunition in an argument later. Dan was a safe audience, and it didn't matter because he was barely listening.

"I hear you, man," Dan opined as he tilted back a shot of whiskey and nodded as he swallowed. "You know, I never made it stick either with women. They ain't happy leavin' things the way they are, right?"

Rick was trying to figure out what he meant by this, and then he elaborated.

"I mean, listen, I've had at least 40 girls that loved me and I never lived with one of them. They really loved me. And I loved them back. Now, I don't mean to say anything bad…" He paused dramatically to take a long swig of beer. "The thing is, they always wanted to get serious and move in together. They never want to stay neutral. They just don't think like men. We're happy when things are good, right?"

"Yes, sure," Rick said. "You mean things always broke off when you didn't profess your love? In the very least a woman will eventually want you to say, 'I only want you,' right?"

"Yeah. Like that," he said dubiously. "I mean, they don't ever just want to keep things the way they are, right? Keep it good like it is in the beginning. They want to get serious. Change it all. That's why I'm glad it's just me out there in Seaford. You know?"

Dan's voice had an angry edge now, and Rick was trying to picture the lineup of 40 or so women that were madly in love with him only to have their hopes dashed. Merv had been standing nearby washing glasses and didn't seem to be paying attention but glanced up now with a stern look in his eye.

"When you're with a woman, you either love her or you don't. If you don't, move on. When she doesn't love you, you try a little harder unless you love yourself more than her. Then, if you're in luck, another woman will come along, and you can try it all out again."

"Once again you've got it right, Merv," Rick said as he raised his glass.

"It's simple," Merv said as he wiped down the bar. "Why go on and on complainin' about it?"

Fredo shifted around on his stool patting each of his pockets nervously, and Dan was busy pulling the label off of his beer bottle.

"My wife likes to track me," Fredo blurted out. "That's why I always change my behavior every day. Don't always do the same thing. They'll get you that way for sure. Don't ever do the same thing every day. You gotta make 'em wonder, right?" Fredo patted his temple with his glasses to emphasize the confusion.

"That's not a bad idea," Rick mumbled as he scanned the wall behind the bar trying to avoid eye contact.

There was a brass plaque he'd never noticed with a dragon image on a crest and the words: "Facilis venire. Facilis exire."

"Easy come, easy go," he said out loud.

Fredo was back to his racing form, and Dan had gone to the bathroom. Merv looked at Rick and gave him a nod. "All good. You're all set?"

"Yeah, thanks Merv. I should get going."

"Alright then, don't be a stranger. You're one of the nicest of my customers. You never give me a problem."

He said this with uncharacteristic tenderness as he walked to the back of the bar and smiled over his shoulder while making a few more exaggerated stabs at the blank television screen.

Rick walked out squinting into the late afternoon light that gleamed across the Hudson and chuckled as he paused to put on his sunglasses.

"Funny how that's what everyone says about me," he thought. "Why am I always the 'nice guy' to everyone?"

When Claire broke it off with him for the last time she said he was too nice, and he had tried to reason with her asking, "Don't you want a man who will love and respect you, take care of you if you need it?"

"No," Claire had answered plainly. "That's not what I'm used to, and it's not the way I am. I need someone to be the man."

Rick walked on thinking about that stinging comment, and the wind at his back off of the river reminded him of the commutes to and from Hoboken. Whether she was with him or not, he felt like a piece of scenery standing on the deck of the ferry watching everyone. There was a mix of single people, couples, and a group of young men whose wives were usually waiting for them with strollers at the dock as if he'd come aboard to witness another generation. He thought he had gotten over Claire, but this memory was right there hanging on the breeze.

"Facilis venire. Facilis exire. Facilis venire…"

He had found a new mantra as he descended the stairs at the corner of King and Varick streets.

"Time for something new," he said as he pushed through the turnstile to board the uptown 1 train.

Chapter 6

Pippa was curled up sleeping on the brown bean bag chair in the corner of the secret room almost completely camouflaged except for his little black nose poking above the edge. Rick had been looking into the mysterious case of Edward Ridley for nearly two hours, and he realized he had only scratched the surface.

The yellowed newspaper sat in front of him on the desk, and several old articles from the early 30s were on the four large monitors with headlines blaring in block type. One full-page piece had a detailed headline that summarized the case above illustrated cutaway views of the scene:

"Perfect Murder Mystery" is a Real Life Detective Story with 65 Detectives: It's Not Lack of Clues, But The Abundance of Them, That Baffles Sleuths Seeking Key to Killing of Rich Edward A. Ridley and Two Secretaries in Sub-Cellar Counting Room

"The police had 65 detectives assigned to this case, and they still couldn't solve it?"

Rick had just spoken for the first time in hours, and Pippa was startled awake struggling to extricate himself.

"What do you think, Pip?"

He dragged his rear legs out and leapt onto Rick's lap in a fluid motion to nuzzle under the flap of his untucked shirt.

"You can't hide from the truth, pal. It's out there," he whispered. "Maybe we should put on your detective coat, and you can sniff out this case?"

The phone had been ringing on the desk, and there was a message from Luisa who ran an agency that had placed him at several freelance jobs. Her tone was positive as usual.

"Hello, Rick!! Can you call me before you go to the office on Tuesday?"

He knew what that meant, and he called her back.

"Hi, Luisa! I bet I know what this is about."

"Yes, this current job is over. They love you, of course, but we knew they'd be hiring someone full-time soon. Not surprising. I thought you'd be finished a few months ago, so this was good that it lasted into the spring. I do have good news. We have something that looks promising starting next week for about a month."

"Oh, that's good," he said without thinking, "but if it's OK with you I need a little break. I need to work on something else for a while. Maybe just a short sabbatical."

There was silence, so Rick decided to emphasize his last point. "I mean to say, 'thank you so much,' but I need to take a little break from this, do you know what I mean?"

"I hear you!"

Luisa sounded irritated but still upbeat.

"I'm sorry. I want to be available for you," Rick interrupted trying to dig himself out of the hole. "You know how much I rely on you to find me these situations. I don't want you to think I'm ungrateful, but I can't keep going without a break."

"I know what you mean, Rick, but this is the reality, and we have to deal with it," she said flatly.

"That's just it. I don't think I want to live in that reality right now."

He intended it to sound like a joke, but the comment had an edge of anger and finality that he didn't try to temper. He had worked consistently, striving to further his career along the way, but something was missing. He sensed he was wasting time that was beginning to run out. It had also become difficult to convince management to hire him because the bosses were typically his age or younger, and they couldn't understand why he'd want to come in and handle the tasks that they'd worked so hard to put behind them. There were down times and up times, but the satisfaction he'd once felt in the work had gone, and now it was only for the paycheck.

"This is not the answer I needed to hear tonight," Luisa said in an uncharacteristic, high-pitched voice.

"Sorry, to disappoint you," he said apologetically trying to mimic her pained tone. "I just need a month or so."

"OK. No problem! Just let me know when you're ready again," she said ending the call.

Rick cradled the phone in his palm thinking about what he'd just said. He'd never turned down a job, or even a chance at a job, since he was 14. He didn't want her to think he'd given up, and he certainly wasn't ready or able to retire.

"Let's see," he said in an overly cheerful tone, "where were we, Pip? Ah, yes, we were getting ready to solve a mystery."

He sat quietly and gazed absently at the articles spread across the screens trying to put the conversation out of his mind as he followed the dotted lines and arrows in the illustration leading down the stairs to the cellar office. He held Pippa to his chest cradling his head in his hands, and his tongue darted out to lick his cheek. He hated being licked but occasionally let him get away with these little stolen kisses. Pippa jumped off of his lap to curl up at his feet, and Rick turned his full attention back to the monitors.

"Why couldn't they find the murderer? Too many likely suspects perhaps?"

It seemed Ridley had led an unremarkable life from 1901 until the first murder in 1931. Rick could only guess what led up to Moench's violent demise and the double homicide that followed in 1933.

"How do we find out what was going on with Ridley during those last years, Pip? Maybe we need to start at the beginning?"

He searched for everything he could find on Ridley & Sons dry goods store and opened window after window across the screens in front of him sliding them around like a puzzle, his eyes darting back and forth trying to make sense of it all.

"This is going to take a while," he sighed as Pippa snored lightly at his feet.

There were census records, articles, and store advertisements to read. He printed a detailed landmark designation report that had been written about the remaining portion of store building still standing on the Orchard St. side along Grand St. and sat down on the bean bag chair. It wasn't long before his eyes started to close.

Rick dreamed he and Claire were walking down the beach together. They were talking and laughing, and the water was sparkling blue. He bent down to pick up a shell and turned around to hand it to her, but she wasn't there anymore. There was only an old man slowly walking away. He was holding an umbrella under his arm and wore a long coat, galoshes, and a black, wide-brimmed hat. His wispy, white beard blew side to side in the breeze. Rick tried to call out for Claire, but he couldn't make a sound. The old man continued to shuffle away, and he stood on the sand alone.

Chapter 7

Monday morning got off to an early start at 5 a.m. with Pippa nudging and then licking his foot which was always guaranteed to wake him.

"OK, boy," he said yawning. "Good morning little guy. We have to stop falling asleep in here. My back is killing me."

His leg bumped the desk as he stood up, and the four monitors sprang to life.

"Well, it's a good thing I have nowhere to go this week. Lots of work to do and not a paycheck in sight."

Carolina would be there in the early afternoon, so he planned to take Pippa for a long walk later to avoid the vacuum. After he poured himself some coffee, and the dog went underneath the couch for his morning nap, he was back in the secret room scanning everything he'd pulled up the night before.

As he sat trying to absorb the array of material, he suddenly remembered the dream and felt a sickening sadness wash over him. It was Ridley walking away on the beach. He was dressed exactly as described in the article Uncle Will saved for him.

"It's not Claire I need to find," he said rubbing his eyes. "I need to find Ridley."

Despite Rick's interest in New York history he'd never heard of Ridley & Sons. It was the "CHEAP STORE" according to their ads, competing on price and the sheer magnitude of their selection in the same eight-column newspaper space with the likes of A.T. Stewart and W.H. Macy & Co., and the growth of their business was exponential.

The elder Edward Ridley was born in Newark, England in 1819. Educated as a lawyer, he decided to become a dry goods merchant instead but then closed his store in 1843 after debts grew too high. He packed up his wife and two young sons, Edward and Arthur, and emigrated to Albany, NY to start over. Things went much better for the American Ridleys, and he operated two successful stores, one in Albany and another in Saratoga. The family relocated to Manhattan a few years later leasing space at 311$^{1/2}$ Grand St. near the corner of Allen St.

This was a main crosstown thoroughfare, and the location was also easily accessible from neighborhoods to the north and south with the Second Avenue El trains stopping near the door. The structure at the southeast corner of Grand and Allen was capped by a dome with a large flag to signal train riders they'd arrived at the stop for Ridley's, and the business soon expanded to adjoining buildings. Less than 10 years later Ridley & Sons had annexed almost the entire block with the various departments spread across open floor space divided by columns and adjoining doorways. With this success the family residence moved from the top of the wholesale department at 66 Allen St. to a large estate in Gravesend, Brooklyn. The growth continued, and several more buildings along Grand, Allen, and Orchard streets were acquired. Ridley & Sons was more like a modern mall than a single store. They employed thousands and delivered by wagon across the city.

By the time the elder Ridley passed away unexpectedly in 1883, plans should have already been made to move the store's location to a more popular shopping district. Macy's had already moved to 14th St. and Sixth Ave., and A.T. Stewart had built a shopping mecca at Broadway and 10th St. The times had changed, but the Ridleys had not. Some ads acknowledged the fact that the store was out of the way but quickly pointed out that the sheer quantity, quality, and low prices more than made up for any inconvenience. References to "cheap" in the headline or anywhere else in the ads had disappeared by 1885 once the two brothers took over. They made a few costly improvements to the superstore they'd created, and then things seemed to be status quo for the Ridley brothers until they closed the store and sold off all of the assets in 1901. The neighborhood itself had changed over the years from single-family homes to tenements filled with newer immigrants. Everything around them was changing, but the Ridley brothers' business plan had always stayed the same.

With this split, the brothers dissolved the dream of their father along with his life's work, and they appear to have gone separate ways. There was little else to read about Albert, but Edward seemed to have become a strange, miserly hermit who was happy to count his money in his subterranean cave. Of course, it was difficult for anyone to discern the real Edward Ridley from the sensational portrait of him presented after the murders.

"This is where Moench and Weinstein intersect," Rick thought. "They were both dealing with the cash as it was coming and going. They touched everything. They were in a perfect position to embezzle from Ridley. Could that be why Moench was killed and Weinstein stepped in? Keep it all in the family? Weinstein's brother was managing the garage above the sub-cellar office. He would have heard the shots, perhaps? Maybe one of the Weinsteins came running and saw old Ridley standing over the body?"

He sat in the big swivel chair looking back and forth between screens and made quick notes on a pad in his lap.

"This could be getting juicier, Pip."

Pippa barked twice dismissively and left the room with his nails clicking away on the staircase as he started to bark more excitedly. Carolina had arrived, and by the time he made it down the stairs to greet her Pippa was already being held to her chest, his head gyrating ecstatically as he darted his tongue out trying to lick her neck and face.

"Yes," Rick thought, "the little guy has the right idea."

"Hi. Good to see you, Carolina. Boy, he really loves you. He gets so excited. Sorry about that."

"That's OK, Rick. I love this little guy," she gushed.

It always sounded so intimate when she called him "Rick," as if it was a secret that she was calling him that.

"Maybe Ian told her to call me Mr. Gordon? That would be just like him," he thought, and then he said, "Well, we're going out for a little while. Be back soon. That is if it's OK with you, Pip?"

Pippa looked at Rick with a side glance then back into Carolina's eyes, and he melted into her arms trying to wrap his head behind her neck.

"Yeah, I didn't think I was much competition."

"Oh, Rick, you know this little Pippie loves you so much, too."

"I know. Thanks, Carolina. He obviously has good taste when it comes to you at least," he said laughing.

Rick reached out to pet him and accidentally touched her cheek gently.

"Well, I think it's time we both got out of your hair," he said trying to hide his embarrassment.

They both blushed, and Carolina was flustered. Rick felt like he just threw a ball through a neighbors' window.

"OK. Let's go out for a bit, Pip," he said as he awkwardly attempted to take him out of Carolina's arms, but Pippa pulled his head away and tucked in closer to her in defiance.

Their eyes were close as Rick leaned to reach for Pippa, and they each knew in that moment that this wouldn't work. It couldn't work. They might not even like each other, and they'd never find out. People make quick decisions like that every day without realizing it.

"You know what, Carolina, people talk about forks in the road, but they rarely occur at the right time in life," he said talking at the floor.

"I agree, Rick. I'm sure we're both looking for something about the same. You seem like a good man. A nice man. You deserve someone good. Someone who will appreciate your goodness. Your gentleness."

Rick cringed at this as she reached up and touched the side of his face with the back of her hand. He knew they wouldn't be together, but he was about to kiss her. Her lips were close as he saw her reach out to touch him, but then he felt a light, sisterly tap on his shoulder, and he knew the moment was over.

"Thanks, Carolina. Means a lot to me. You're a real peach yourself."

She gave him a funny look.

"I mean that I feel the same way about you, and I hope you find someone who deserves you."

Carolina smiled as she cupped his face and kissed his cheek. She picked up her bags and walked up the stairs as Rick stood by the door holding the harness in his hand while Pippa jumped against his leg and whined. After a little wrangling, they were out the door and down the steps, but

Pippa kept looking back as they made their way slowly up the street.

"No one's coming, old pal," he said quietly. "It's just us."

Chapter 8

The morning sun streamed across the bed, and Pippa started whimpering and kicking Rick in the side with his rear legs. It was later than usual, and there were a few missed calls from Amanda. She didn't leave a message, but there was a text.

Hey, Gordie. Come to the country with me. I'm leaving tomorrow. Seriously, I need this. I'll pick you up. It's just my cousin's house in Jersey. Relax.

"Hmm," he muttered half awake, "what's this?"

Amanda often conscripted friends for unplanned road trips that usually didn't benefit any of the attendees except her. Sometimes things worked out well for everyone, but it was only coincidental.

Rick replied to her text: *OK, but I'll need to bring Pip.*

Amanda was outside the townhouse at 11:30 the next morning with the top down waving like the queen as she tapped the horn.

"That's a dramatic entrance," Rick said as he grabbed his bag and Pippa's carrier off of the stoop.

"Alright you boys," she said in a babyish voice as Pippa jumped into her lap, "are you ready for an adventure in the country?"

"Just hand him to me when you can't take it anymore," he said. "He'll probably just sleep on your thigh."

"Not to worry, Gord. We're all going to take it easy for a few days. No stress."

"Why exactly are you off from work now and going to stay at your cousin's house?"

Rick liked to ask questions during these impromptu trips especially when there was a conspicuous lack of explanation.

"Oh," she said matter of factly, "it's just a chance for us to hang out. Rob's away for a couple of weeks, and he asked if I could check on the house for him. He said I should go enjoy myself. There's fishing. You can walk down to the stream, and he has everything you need there."

"Well that's good, since I didn't bring a rod or tackle. What are you fishing for? You didn't answer my question. It's Wednesday. I'm out of work right now, but what's your excuse?"

"Taking a few personal days. I'm allowed to do that. Also, by the way, I recently hooked up with Dennis."

Amanda had dated Dennis off and on during the 20 or so years since they'd met in college, and she had broken it off with him each time because he cheated on her.

"OK. That's surprising I guess," Rick said dubiously, "but why are we here now together driving to New Jersey if you're back with him? Why didn't you take him with you instead?"

"He's in Chicago this week. It's hard to explain. I'm not sure how to explain."

Amanda rarely showed her true emotions, or at least she always tried to conceal them with varying levels of success, but now there was a tear in her eye and her lip was quivering.

"I'm pregnant. I think."

Rick's mouth hung open.

"What do you mean, 'you think'?"

"I don't know. I missed my period."

"But, how did this happen?"

There was a moment of silence, and they both laughed uproariously at the same time. It was the kind of belly laugh they'd shared many times for many different reasons. They loved to laugh together, and Rick was slapping her knee.

"But I don't want it!!"

Amanda stopped laughing abruptly as she said this and started to cry. Rick kept patting her leg gently the way his mother always did when he was upset as a child, and then he also started to cry.

"Let's not worry about it right now," she said, pulling herself together when she saw him getting upset.

"OK. We can talk about it another time," he said.

They both focused on the road until it was time to exit. Her cousin's property was in Tewksbury on five or six acres along the Rockaway Creek. They turned down a single-lane road and then down a gravel drive past a small grove of apple trees. She had teased the trip saying that they'd be staying in a historic house. The property had two separate buildings along with a four-car carriage house and a pole barn. There was a main house and a separate summer kitchen that Rob's wife had been using as a painting studio. She had left him the year before after about 25 years. Rick looked in the window as he got out of the car, and the room was empty except for an easel and a stool pushed up against the huge fireplace.

Rick opened the door and Pippa sprang out running quickly around the house and stopping to sniff around the foundation underneath the small, wooden porch.

"What do you think?! Pretty nice," Amanda said. "Old and cool, right?"

Walking in the front door, Rick could tell it had been extensively remodeled over the years but kept close to the original materials and style.

"Yes, this is great. It's incredible. I'd love to have a place like this."

"Wait until you see the other house. It has a huge fireplace where they used to cook. And the property down by the river is beautiful. You're never going to want to leave."

Amanda talked fast and seemed happy now as she put away some of the groceries she'd packed. They sat facing each other on the couch talking for a while. Rick didn't want to mention anything until Amanda brought it up again, and it didn't take very long.

"So," she said letting out a long exaggerated breath, "like I said, I may be preggers. Not sure what's happening."

"I hate to ask the obvious question, but did you do a test?"

"Not yet. I want to wait it out. This country jaunt is my gestation period. I'm going to do it when we get back to the city."

"Sounds non-scientific and not very prudent given the huge glass of vodka you just poured yourself. Who am I to judge, though," Rick said as he poured himself a glass. "Are you sure it's Dennis? Sorry. Probably another stupid question."

"I just haven't been feeling right for the last week, and missing my period coincides perfectly with one rather drunken and unsatisfying night with him. Also, I haven't been near any other semen. Get it?"

"Yeah, I think I saw that filmstrip in fifth grade."

Amanda tilted her glass back and dramatically slammed it on the coffee table.

"OK. So, like I said, I don't think I want a baby. I'm too old for this. It's not my thing. Not anymore. Maybe three years ago."

She stopped talking as she walked to the kitchen, filled her glass with ice again, and topped it off with vodka. Rick wanted to inquire why three years ago would have been better, but instead he blurted out, "Amanda, I love you and will be there for you no matter what happens."

They both laughed at the unintentional cliché.

"I tell you what, Mr. Gordon, you go catch us some fish for dinner, and maybe I'll let you be my unborn baby's fake father."

Rick finished his drink and gave Amanda a kiss on the cheek.

"Anything for the future mother of my possibly fake child. You need to keep up your strength," he said as he leaned over and gave her a firm kiss on the cheek. "Where do you think he keeps the gear?"

"It's out there in the garage," Amanda yawned.

He took Pippa in his arms and walked out the side door then put him down to run a little. The carriage barn was large and meticulously kept with barely any clutter. There was a hay loft and a small-windowed room at the top of a narrow staircase, and an array of fresh-water fishing equipment lined the wall. He looked everything over and took one of the smaller rods, a pair of tall rubber boots, a net, and a tackle box.

"C'mon, Pip, want an early dinner?"

Pippa turned around to look in Rick's direction, and there was a moment of stunned silence before he ran right past him out the door and back up the hill to the house. He was waiting on the front step panting and hopping on his hind legs when Rick caught up.

"Hungry, are you?"

Pippa ate quickly and curled up on the couch. He could hear the shower running and didn't want to disturb Amanda, so he left quietly.

The property sloped past another small grove of trees with a park bench under them, and a narrow footpath continued down to the creek bed. He walked along carefully to guide the rod through the low brush.

The creek was in sight now, and there was a small embankment with a rut worn into it. Instead of his usual cautious manner, he decided to take one large step down into the rut rather than bracing himself against the incline, and suddenly he was laying against the bank with his head next to a rock and his leg tucked at a right angle behind him.

"Good fall. Good fall this time, Ricky. Unscathed," he muttered as he picked himself up.

The first fall was enough to make him cautious, so he walked deliberately along the bank, stepping into the stream to slide past the outgrowth and large boulders. He knew himself too well. Accidents tended to happen in cascades.

He stopped by a bend where there was a pool between a fallen tree and some rocks and put down the net and tackle box. He saw the roof of the pole barn and realized he'd wandered at least 100 yards downstream. There was a small, silver spinner already tied on the line, so he aimed a few casts into the pool to try his luck. He had to reel it in carefully to avoid getting snagged on submerged branches and rocks.

After a few casts Rick could hear footsteps in the water coming his way. At first he couldn't see anything except the shadow of an outstretched arm and hand in the distance waving in the glare of the sunlight and then another fisherman came into full view as he came around the bend downstream. Rick waved back as he smiled and fingered the rod nervously wondering if he had wandered onto his private property. As the man got closer Rick could tell he was smiling, and that put him at ease.

"How's it going?" Rick said as he tucked his rod under his arm preparing to shake his hand. The man stayed a few paces away holding his rod and net in front of him with both hands.

"Fine, fine. Fine day," he said warmly. "I wasn't sure you could see me turning the corner. Didn't want to alarm you. It's turned into a fine day for fishing."

The man looked down at the stream, and the reflection of the sun in the water projected swirls and ripples of golden light on his face.

"Yes, I'm just visiting with a friend, and it's my first dip in the water here. It's the old house up that way," Rick said pointing.

"Ah, sure, that's Rob's place. His wife used to paint and sell her pictures at the craft fair in Oldwick. Nice woman."

The man had a familiar tone but a faraway look in his eye. His beard was all grey from his sideburns down, but his hair was almost completely black when he took off his hat. They both stood looking down at the stream.

"That's nice," Rick said. "It's my first time here, so I don't know. I've never met Rob or his wife. Seems like a great spot, though. Do you have any idea about the history of the house?

"Nope, I don't think I can tell you. Just that it didn't start out in that spot. It was a miller's house. There was a grist mill near here during the revolution. The old timer up that way could tell you all about it. He'd know everything," he said as he pointed toward a small house on the opposite bank.

Rick hadn't noticed it before because he was so concerned about his footing. The house looked abandoned, but wisps of smoke rose from the chimney.

"OK, thanks, maybe I'll run into him while I'm here," he said hopefully.

"Not likely. He's dead."

"Oh, that's too bad," Rick laughed nervously.

"Well, from what I heard, old John brought it on himself. Lived up there alone for nearly 20 years after his wife died. I think he took to drinking more than what's festive and social if you know what I mean, but he sure loved history."

He looked at Rick directly in the eyes for the first time and said, "What good is history if there's nobody to share the present with you?"

The words "with you" hung in the air as if he'd directed them at Rick, and then he looked down at the stream again and continued with a lighter tone.

"You could see him down here early in the morning and around sundown. Right around now, I guess. He used to say the big ones bite at sundown. Sometimes he'd yell or whistle at the fish to come up, but I'm not sure that's the way to do it. These fish here are skittish. Can't force 'em on. You need the proper touch."

"I guess that's half the battle," Rick said.

"That's the only thing, my boy. The rest is just flash. You also need the right tackle. That spinner you have there is OK, but switch to a rooster tail if you really want to hook one for dinner tonight."

"OK, thanks a lot," Rick said as he opened up the small box of lures and pulled out one with silver beads and a treble hook inside a light yellow, feathered tip.

"Try dropping it in over there around that bend," he said pointing downstream. "There's a nice hole there just beyond a fallen tree." As he began to walk slowly away he turned again quickly and said, "There's one out there for you. Might not set your hook today, but that's why we fish, right?"

He turned away without waiting for an answer, and Rick stood holding the lure between his fingers waving vaguely as he watched him deftly clamber away up the middle of the rocky stream bed without slipping at all.

"Thank you! I didn't catch your name," Rick stammered as he watched the old timer easily negotiate the slippery rocks.

"It's John," he said over his shoulder.

"Rick. Nice to meet you, John."

The sound of the stream seemed to increase, and John didn't turn around. He was waving his arm as he walked away, and then Rick heard him loudly whistling his favorite bluegrass song.

Lord preserve us and protect us, we've been drinking whiskey 'fore breakfast…

"Maybe I'll see you again!" Rick yelled over the sound of the whistling and rushing stream.

The background noise subsided suddenly, and John turned to look back in Rick's direction. "You might," he said brightly and then continued to whistle loudly as he walked upstream.

We've been drinking whiskey 'fore breakfast…

Rick picked up the net, made his way around the gravelly bend, and saw the downed tree. There was a muddy, high spot on the bank with a good angle at the pool. He stood for a few moments listening, but he couldn't hear the whistling anymore, and he looked around and took in his surroundings for the first time. It was a peaceful place. The creek took a sharp curve around a bend here and rolled over some low rocks making a rippling, gurgling sound. It was the kind of sound they used to put on relaxation tapes and fancy alarm clocks. There was an oak tree on the other bank that had some of its dry leaves from last season whispering in the slight breeze, refusing to be cast aside. Rick admired that resilience.

He shivered slightly which made it more difficult to tie on the lure. The thin, low-test line and his cold fingers made the process laborious with several false starts on the knot. He stood holding the lure, dangling it in front of him and shaking it slightly after dipping it into the water, then opened the bail and made a quick flick of his wrist toward the spot John pointed out.

The line was slack for a moment as he began reeling slowly. After two or three turns it felt slack again and then tight as the rod tip bent. There was a flash at the surface, and he reeled in slowly around the half sub-merged tree. It was a brown trout at least 11 inches long, its tail curled, pushing against the hoop of the net as Rick held it gently just below the surface of the water. The fish wasn't struggling anymore, just calmly, slowly moving in the net.

He held it there for a moment and said, "Today's not your day, fish," then gently pulled out the hook, lowered the net into a deeper spot, and watched the trout swim back into the current.

The sun had gone down quickly, and it was already hard to see the path back to the house by the time Rick made his way upstream. He went to the carriage house to drop off the rod and tackle box and wore the rubber boots back to the side landing where he'd left his shoes. He could hear Pippa barking inside and hoped that he hadn't been doing that the entire time he was gone. Amanda was standing in the doorway wearing flannel pajamas and tapping her bare foot.

"Well, I don't see any dinner in your hands, Gordo. Failed again at your manly duties?"

"Nah, I just had a couple of nibbles. It was good, though. I only fell once."

"Hmmm, that's not like you. Why are you not covered in contusions, thorns, and fish hooks?"

"Just my lucky day, I guess," he said smiling as he took off his coat and poured himself a glass. "Looks like we're going to need another bottle, my dear Amanda."

"I brought two bottles, my dear Richard," she retorted in a bad British accent.

She passed him a small wooden pipe, and they sat on the floor by the fire blowing the smoke up the chimney.

"I think you need to get back on the horse, Rick."

There was a pause. Amanda only used his regular name when she wasn't kidding around. It was a signal that he should pay close attention to what she was saying.

"Excuse me. I didn't realize there were horses here. Where does Rob keep them?"

"You know what I mean. You need to go on a date. Meet someone. Get back in your groove. Enjoy life again."

"What the hell gave you the impression that I wasn't enjoying life?"

Rick was getting irritated already because Amanda had entered her "I know you better than you" lecture mode. There would be no more equitable repartee tonight. Rick listened to Amanda, shut her down wherever possible, and hoped she would get tired soon.

"Listen to me, Mr. Gordon. You don't know what's good for you. You've proven that fact over and over."

Amanda was slurring, which Rick used to think was cute when they were in high school, but it had gotten more nasty and desperate sounding

30 years later. It meant the evening was effectively over except for the formalities.

"You need to take out my new friend at work," Amanda said breathlessly as if she were running out of oxygen before she could finish the sentence.

"Do I?"

Rick was glaring at her and felt completely sober now as he awaited her final blow.

"Yes, she's a new paralegal at the office, but she's like a friend, you know?"

"OK," he said calmly. "You remind me about it tomorrow, and we'll get something set up."

"Good boy," Amanda said in a motherly voice as she patted his cheek and turned to the side to collapse onto the couch.

She was asleep and started to snore almost immediately. Rick put his backpack on his shoulder and walked quietly up the creaking stairs with Pippa in his arms hoping he wouldn't wake her and that the blind date promise he'd made would be forgotten by morning.

Chapter 9

"Who wants eggs and bacon?!"

Pippa jumped up and barked excitedly under the sheets as he deftly extricated himself from between Rick's legs. Amanda had woken up almost as soon as she laid down and couldn't get back to sleep, so she was the first one at the general store when it opened at 7 a.m.

Rick carried Pippa down the narrow staircase and turned to see Amanda in an apron whisking a large bowl of eggs. She looked perfectly fine. No one would have known she'd polished off a large amount of vodka and was probably awake most of the night. She had a unique resilience.

"Well, you look chipper, Ms. Colville. Up early this morning were you?"

"Yes," she said in a bubbly voice, "and you get to reap the benefits of my insomnia. Bon appétit!"

Rick fed Pippa while Amanda put eggs, bacon, and toast on their plates.

"So, we need to get this date planned," she said matter of factly.

Rick bumped his head on the edge of the countertop as he stood up. "Sure! Let's do this," he said enthusiastically as he rubbed his head.

"OK. I don't have a picture that does her justice, but look at this."

She held up her phone, and there was a blurry photo of a blonde woman smiling. That was all that Rick could make out.

"Alright," he said dubiously. "That's not telling me much, but I'm happy to meet her since I told you I would. Should we send her a blurry photo of me so that she can also take part in this decision?"

"Very funny, El Gordo. She's perfectly lovely unlike you. You'll be glad I set you two up when you get married, and you can start thanking me by making me your best woman."

"Slow down there! Don't go laying claim to my future happiness before I even have a chance to smile about it."

"I just want you to be happy," she said in an exaggerated, pouty voice.

"OK, then please stop using that voice. I'll go on a date, but don't get all crazy talking about a wedding."

Amanda ignored him as she picked up her phone.

"I'm sending her your number and telling her you're expecting her call."

"Boy, we've come a long way, I guess. I don't even have to ask the girl out? I don't need to call first and tell her I'm interested?"

"You just need to shut up and go out with her."

Amanda was eating with one hand and texting with the other while Rick finished his eggs and drank the last of his coffee. He walked around the room looking closely at the hand-hewn beams and ran his fingers along the chiseled surfaces.

"I met a guy out on the stream yesterday who said this house was moved to this location. I wonder if Rob knows the history of the place?"

"Well, I can text him and ask. He's definitely into the history here. Hold on."

He poured another cup of coffee and looked out the window at the grove of trees and the path leading down to the creek.

"It was strange," he said. "He told me about a guy named John who lived on the other side of the creek, but he died. Then I asked him his own name, and he told me his name was John."

"What are you saying, mental case? John is a very common name in case you didn't know. Do you think you saw a ghost?"

Amanda laughed and jumped around waving her arms making eery sounds.

"I'm just saying it was a little odd now that I think of it," he said calmly.

Amanda's phone chimed with Rob's response.

"Yes," she said as she read the message. "He says the house was originally closer to the road. The owner had a grist mill during the revolution. Boy, how do you guys not know each other. Isn't there some kind of society of history nerds?"

"Ask Rob about the old guy across the creek who passed away."

"What do you want me to ask him, Detective Columbo?"

Rick ignored her as he walked into a room off of the kitchen that Rob had set up as a small office. It had a low entryway framed by 6x6 beams, and he had to duck his head to enter. He felt his face flush when he saw a picture of John on the desk. He was standing by the grove of trees next to another man who Rick assumed was Rob based on the other photos. Each man was smiling widely and holding a large brown trout. He brought it back to the kitchen, grabbed Amanda's phone, and took a picture of it.

"Ask him if this is his neighbor John who passed away."

Amanda hit send and typed quickly.

"He says 'Yes, that's John. How did you know?' Holy crap, Rick. You have to be kidding me."

A wave of excitement ran through him. It wasn't happiness, vindication, or a thrill. He hadn't felt this way since he heard his parents had been killed. Rick was 10 years old when his Uncle Will came to the house while his parents were out to dinner. The babysitter was crying, and he didn't know why. His uncle told him on the way home in the car, and Rick only remembered crying for the rest of the night after that. He felt dazed as he stood holding the photo and staring toward the creek and finally said, "Am I losing my mind? Did I see this photo before I went fishing and imagine it all?"

Amanda looked at him with actual interest for the first time in a while and said, "What does this mean?"

"Not sure, but I had a conversation with him down in the creek yesterday, and he told me what lure to use and where to catch a fish."

"Some ghostly angler! You didn't catch a thing," she said scoffingly.

"That's the thing, he told me I might not hook the right one. I went where he said, and I caught a really nice one, but it was as if he was standing there over my shoulder telling me it wasn't the one, so I let it go."

For once, Amanda was speechless while they both sat at the table and looked out the window.

"Well, I think you're weird," she said finally.

"You're a weirdo, too," he said accusingly. "Let's take a walk down to the creek."

Pippa was running in tight circles using his staccato squeaks to make sure everyone knew it was time for a walk while Rick and Amanda scrambled to put on their shoes and coats.

It was beautifully crisp and cold and officially springtime, but the biting wind made it feel more like a winter morning as they walked down the slope. Amanda was rolling her eyes and complaining right away, and Pippa bounded down the hill, running up and down doubling his effort, as they followed slowly.

"I just want to go down here and take a look at John's house. We need to walk a little bit further."

"OK, whatever you say, Agent Mulder."

"You're no Dana Scully," he shot back over his shoulder as they walked single file through a narrow part of the path.

Pippa ran ahead down to the stream bed and barked in the direction of John's house. Rick looked at the chimney, but there was no smoke, and he stood staring down at the water.

"You forgot your rod, bass master," she said in a bored voice breaking the silence.

Pippa had run downstream along the bank and disappeared around the bend, and Rick went after him calling his name. He was barking excited-ly sitting back on his haunches in the same spot where Rick had caught the trout. As Rick got a little closer, he suddenly stopped barking and looked up as if someone were patting his head. He held that pose pant-ing happily until Rick finally reached him and clicked on his leash.

"OK, Pip. Let's go back now," he said as looked around.

Pippa anchored himself in the gravelly soil looking up to the sky as Rick reached to pull him away.

"C'mon now, Pip. Let's go," Rick whispered as he scooped him up to carry him back. He looked up at John's house again, and it seemed more empty and a little more run down today. Amanda was standing at the path along the bank with her hands on her hips.

"Well, did you two find your special new friend?"

Rick was carefully walking along the stream edge because he had forgotten to wear the rubber boots. He shook his head to say, "stop," but Amanda wasn't done yet.

"Do you think we should call in a paranormal team?"

"OK, enough," he said quickly. "I know what I saw and heard. I don't care if you believe it."

They walked back to the house without discussing it further, and Rick got Pippa cleaned up on the side landing.

"How do you manage to get so dirty? My little lowrider picks everything up along the way, huh?"

Pippa was shimmying and shaking as Rick poured water over his underbelly and legs and wiped him clean. By the time they got inside, Amanda was standing by the kitchen counter tapping her foot again.

"You're good here, right? We don't need to stay. I'm good if you're ready to go."

Rick was taken aback for a moment but glad to hear she wanted to leave. He wasn't ready to fish again after what he'd experienced, and he was hoping Amanda would go home and see a doctor or take a pregnancy test before she polished off any more vodka.

"No, of course, we can leave whenever you want," he said. "I've had my fill of the country for now. Say the word, and I'll get ready to go."

Pippa heard this and began jumping against Amanda's legs. They were on the road back to the city before lunch.

"You can take my friend out now that we're back," Amanda said slyly as they emerged from the Holland Tunnel.

"Alright, sure. Is she available tonight? I thought I was waiting for her to make the move. When is the Sadie Hawkins dance?"

"Gordon, what the hell are you talking about? What is a Sadie Hawkins dance? You know, this is one of the reasons you're single. You say strange things."

"Forget it," he said dryly. "Just have her give me a call."

Chapter 10

Rick and Pippa had been back at home for a few hours when Amanda called. She usually texted, so Rick answered immediately.

"Hello? This is not your sushi delivery number."

"Shut up, smart ass. Are you ready to go out tonight? Go out with Rebecca?"

"Are you a pimp? Why are you pushing this so much? Also, this is the first time you've told me her name. Why do you seem to be slowly revealing details."

"I'm revealing your future bride to you," Amanda said loudly.

"OK. Don't shout. It does not become a gentile woman like you. She really wants to meet me somewhere tonight, or are you the one pushing it?"

"Not just anywhere, Gordie. Take her to the tapas place near you."

This sounded like "topless place" to Rick which meant Amanda had probably dipped into the sauce a little bit when she got home.

"The place on Sixth?"

"Yes. Do it."

"OK. What time? Does she have that blurry picture of me yet so that we'll know each other?"

"You'll know her when you see her. She's gorgeous. Plus I described you to her. Don't overthink it."

"No, I wouldn't want to overthink this. You're right. That would be a mistake. It wouldn't be prudent…"

Amanda hung up on him, and he still didn't have any contact information or anything else to go on besides a vague recollection of a blurry face that may or may not have belonged to his future bride Rebecca.

Then Amanda texted: *Meet her there at 7. Don't be a dork and let me down. As usual.*

He tossed the phone onto the bed and said, "Alright, Pip, I guess it's time for me to get all dolled up."

Pippa looked at Rick briefly but turned away to continue tearing the stuffing out from the head of his favorite toy. It was a miniature squirrel holding an acorn, and Rick had several fresh backups in the drawer.

"Yes, I know that's all you need, but I might want a little more than that. Someone I can snuggle up to and chew perhaps? That didn't sound right, but you get the idea, Pip. Although I have no idea what kind of nut I'm about to meet, and you two are already up close and personal. You seem quite content and well suited for each other."

Pippa began to vigorously hump the undersized and defenseless squirrel, and Rick walked out of the room shaking his head. The phone rang again, and this time it was Ian.

"Hey, boss! How are you?!"

There was a lot of street noise in the background, and Ian yelled, "Is this Mr. Gordon, I presume?"

"Yes! How are you, old boy?"

"I'm good, Rick. I may be coming back to see you someday soon, but I'm not sure exactly when."

"Of course! It's your place. Come back when you like, and I'll be out of your way."

"No, I don't need you to leave. I just may have to come back for some legal issues. No big whoop."

Ian had his fingers in so many pies that it wasn't worth asking him if everything was alright. This wasn't the first time he was going to court, and he would let Rick know if he were in some kind of trouble.

"Well, the place is here and ready for your occupancy whenever you return. Pip and I love being here. We're getting used to being caretakers."

"Hey, man, you're my go-to guy. You know how much I trust you. You are a key holder of the domain in perpetuity. You know about the secret room, so now you're in the secret society."

"Yeah, I hope you don't mind, but I dipped into the emergency supply in there."

"Do I mind? I would mind if you hadn't already dipped into it. I'll bet you haven't been looking very hard. It's already past Easter time. Why don't you go peek around and find the eggs I left you?"

Rick went and looked around the room wondering where Ian would have hidden his "eggs" and noticed the row of books on a shelf above the back of the love seat. They blended into the background, and Rick had never paid attention to them.

"I'm getting warmer, I think," Rick said.

"If you know how much I read, you may be able to deduce the hidden location," Ian said mysteriously.

The books were fake and each contained a different variety.

"All is well. I've discovered your numerous genres of literature," Rick whispered.

"Good, Gordon. So what's up? I don't have long. I have to go meet a guy before the market opens."

"I won't keep you. I'm just about to go on a very hastily arranged blind date."

"Arranged by whom?"

"It's Amanda again," Rick said sadly.

"You can do this, man. You will crush this blind date. Where are you going?"

"It's a tapas place near here on Sixth."

"Stick with cheese and cooked food. No cured meat," Ian said with certainty as the background noise increased. "Gotta go, man. See you soon maybe. I'll call."

"OK, bye!"

Knowing that Ian had far-reaching research tentacles he employed to inform his investment strategies, Rick laughed to himself as he wondered if this warning had been based on inside intelligence about tainted ham in the neighborhood. He poured himself a glass of rum as he pondered this and carried it to his bedroom as Pippa trailed behind.

"OK, Pip," he said as he opened the closet door, "what does a guy my age wear to a tapas bar on Thursday night when having drinks and small bites with a blurry, beautiful stranger?"

Pippa responded by jumping into the open underwear drawer and kicking it all up into a ball.

"OK, I think this will do," he said as he pulled a white shirt and a pair of jeans out of the closet.

It was only a short walk, so he took his time as he tried to piece together why he was on his way to a blind date when he thought he'd be relaxing and fishing in New Jersey. He also thought about what he would be doing at that moment if it weren't for Amanda, and he realized he owed her the satisfaction of this set-up.

The restaurant was a few steps down from the sidewalk, and double doors led into a dimly lit space that looked comfortable with its gleaming tiles. There were two-person tables lined along the wall, and he looked around the bar to see if she had arrived.

Then he heard a soft voice in his ear saying, "Rick? You're Rick, right?"

He was standing next to a stunning woman with long, blonde hair and a nervous smile, and he stared for a moment in disbelief.

"Yes! You're Rebecca? Of course! Hello, I'm Rick. Well, I guess you've already picked me out, so there's no point in going on with the introductions…"

"You are cute, Rick. Just like Amanda said."

This compliment threw him off for another moment, and he just smiled nodding his head at her.

"You don't take compliments well, I guess?"

He was still nodding weakly and said, "No. I guess I'm not used to that, or I don't respond well to them. Hmm. Thanks! Sorry, can we please start over?"

Rebecca laughed and said, "Sure."

"OK, great. I promise I'm well versed in all of the usual social graces. It just takes me a few minutes to get rolling sometimes."

Things started to go smoother after that, and they covered the usual points: work, hometown, favorite food, favorite vacation. She seemed slightly uncomfortable as they talked, but he tried to put it out of his mind. After all, they had just met 20 minutes before and been thrust together by Amanda.

"God knows what Amanda told her about me," Rick thought.

Rebecca reached out and touched his hand. "You said you're taking some time off from work? What does that entail exactly?"

"Well, as you might expect, there's very little going to the office in the morning and coming home at night. That stopped immediately."

She seemed genuinely concerned and said, "Very funny. I mean, what are you going to do with yourself?"

"I'm not sure yet," he said as if he'd just realized that he hadn't thought about it at all. "I know it's too early to retire. I'm sure something will come up before I know it. In the meantime, I'm looking forward to doing something different for as long as possible while this lasts."

She stared into his eyes and said, "So, I understand you're quite the history buff?"

He took a sip of his martini as she asked the question and swallowed hard. He hated that expression.

"I don't know about 'buff,' but I suppose Amanda told you that as a warning. She's a 'here and now' person. Actually, since you asked, history is part of what I plan to do with myself. I've been looking into a very interesting, old New York story."

"Oh, that's good," she said blandly as her voice rose slightly to emphasize her next point. "I'm also sort of a 'here and now' kind of person."

"Hey, that's OK with me if it's OK with you," he said as he studied her face for a sign that it was also OK with her.

"Well, I don't want to get all spiritual on you," she said quietly, "but it's not good to dwell on the past. I mean it's not good for your soul. You need your spirit to be free to expand. I've been doing a lot of meditation, and my guide always reminds us in the group to project forward to the future. You could be making yourself really sick…"

Rick had his elbow on the table holding his chin in his hand while he listened and waited for an opening.

"Makes sense, I guess," he said quickly. "Don't they say you get cancer if you hold too much inside? I suppose it is very freeing to ignore the past. I say whatever works for you is great."

"Well, I could go on, but it's a little advanced to jump into since you don't know anything about it yet. You could come to the center after one of my sessions, and I'll introduce you to our guide," Rebecca said as she cut a small piece of octopus and raised it to her mouth.

"Thanks. Yes, yes, thank you," Rick stammered searching for the right words. "I'm not really into that."

"Well, not yet, of course," Rebecca mumbled matter of factly as she nodded and tried to chew, "but we'll get you going right away. We'll get you on the right path."

Rick tilted back his half-full martini and looked at Rebecca smiling. She was still chewing the same piece of octopus and smiling back at him.

"I don't know what it is," Rick thought, "but I like her even if she wants me to join her cult or whatever the hell she's talking about."

"You're such a nice guy," Rebecca said beaming at him. "Amanda told me all about you. You deserve to be happy and not so wrapped up in the past."

Rick was getting irritated quickly but tried to hide it. He wanted to let her have it and tell her that they had nothing in common, that he respected the past because we learn from it and that's what guides us toward the future, that people who turn a blind eye to the past were doomed to repeat the same mistakes. He wanted to recommend she read Santayana. Instead, he gazed steadily at her and smiled. She was very attractive, and she seemed to be attracted to him.

"You know, I never thought of it that way," Rick said as if he were pondering the point. "However, I'm happy the way I am. I do appreciate your concern. Let's not talk about meditation or the future anymore tonight. It's been fun, right? Just being here in the moment right now?"

"Sure, I understand if you're not ready yet," Rebecca said sounding dejected.

They said goodbye on the sidewalk outside the restaurant with a quick peck on the cheek. He turned to walk north as she walked east, and he thought he'd call her and tell her he had a great time, but he still didn't have her number. It wasn't until he was on the stoop again, standing at the front door listening to Pippa trundling down the stairs at full speed barking his serious bark, then whimpering as he jumped and scratched on the door, that Rick realized what had just happened. He was letting himself fall for someone who wasn't right for him. He was doing it again. He was the one failing to learn from the past.

Rick thought about Rebecca telling him how nice he was, and his face burned with a mix of anger and embarrassment.

"I'm not that fucking nice," he said under his breath as he opened the door and knelt down to catch Pippa in his arms.

He held him and walked slowly up the stairs. Pippa wriggled out from his grasp to rest his head on his shoulder and lick his chin, and Rick suddenly felt happier than he'd been in a long time.

"I'm cute, Pip. That's what she said," he whispered in his ear. "Someone cute is out there for both of us, but now it's time for me to get to work."

Chapter 11

The phone was buzzing on the nightstand at 7 a.m. the next morning. Rick had been in the secret room writing until after midnight but had begun making a point of going to bed rather than falling asleep sitting upright in the chair. Pippa made sure he adhered to this new plan by barking at him as soon as he started to slump over, and it had done wonders for Rick's sore back. He stared at the ceiling and rubbed Pippa's belly until the phone stopped vibrating, and a beep alerted him that there was a voice message. This was followed by the sound of texts being delivered. He knew it was Amanda.

He didn't bother looking at the texts or listening to the message and simply called her back.

Amanda yelled, "Hellooo! What do you have to say for yourself?"

"I say 'what the hell is wrong with you?'"

"Rebecca said you guys had a nice time," she deadpanned.

"Yes. It was a nice time," he said in a monotone voice to match Amanda's.

"So, when are you going to go out with her again?!"

"That's the thing. I don't think that's a good idea. She's, well, she's great," he said searching for the right words. "She's really great. A nice woman…"

"What is wrong with you? You have a hot girl who thinks you're hot too," she whined. "You're both single. Why wouldn't you go out with her. You don't have to marry her. I was only kidding about being your woman of honor."

"I know. It's hard to explain, but I just know it's not a good match for me in the long run," he said apologetically.

"You could have fun in the short run. You're too hard on yourself. Loosen up."

"That's great advice for a guy who's a player, my dear Amanda. Anytime I tried to play the game I got burned. Unlike most normal people I would rather be alone than end up in the wrong relationship again. It's all or nothing for me now. I'm doing myself a favor. It's selfish not self destructive."

There was a brief silence, and then Amanda did something he didn't expect. She agreed with him.

"Rick, I just want the best for you. I want you to be happy."

"Thanks," he sighed with relief.

"Oh, now that we have that important matter out of the way, I have big news."

"OK! I wish I had some coffee, but go ahead and hit me with it."

"I'm going to be a mother," she said gently.

Rick felt tears welling up, and he started stammering, "What, wow, OK, great…"

"Calm down there, Ricky! I need you to be calm. Don't start running around cutting up sheets and boiling water."

He stopped short and laughed, "Why did they always do that in the old movies?"

"I don't know why," Amanda laughed. "Can we go back to me, please?"

"Yes, sorry. I got excited."

"I took a test, and it's definitely positive. I still have a long way to go. It should be seven and a half more months to be exact. I need to go to see the lady doctor to confirm, but I threw up this morning, still didn't get my period, feel awful right now, so this must be the happiest time of my life, I guess?"

"Oh, Amanda. Sorry you don't feel well. You can do this."

"Easy for you to say, Gordo. You're not the one with an alien growing inside of you, and you're not the one who has to quit drinking," Amanda chided.

"Good point," Rick conceded.

"So, that's the other reason I'm calling. I won't be seeing you for a while."

"What do you mean?"

"I'm disembarking the fun train. You need to ride it by yourself. It will be too tempting for me to hang out with you. I know myself."

"I've heard pregnant women are turned off by drinking. Something changes inside," Rick offered.

"Well, I'll be seeing you then once I go through the change. Don't worry, I'm always here for you if you need me."

He knew that he couldn't reason with her. They'd had long breaks in contact over the years, but it was always because one or the other was too wrapped up in a relationship. This time it was different, and he selfishly wanted her to be in his life as much as he wanted to be there for her. He was afraid to ask but needed to know.

"What does Dennis think about this?"

"Well, I told him I was probably pregnant with his child, and of course he thought I was joking. I thought about it last night, and I don't want him in my life. I want to raise the child without him as long as he's alright with that. He probably wouldn't last too long before cheating on me anyway. Obviously, he will still be the father. My mind is mush right now. Don't worry about me, though. I'm going to take a nap."

"Well I'm going to have some coffee and try to wake up," Rick said rubbing his eyes. "I'll talk to you soon, OK? Feel better!"

Pippa was squirming around trying to get his attention to no avail.

"She will be a great mother," he thought as he laid on his back staring at a small crack in the ceiling plaster.

Amanda had always talked about having a baby when she was younger but had gradually resigned herself to life as a single, successful woman. He couldn't blame her for feeling confused now that this unplanned miracle had presented itself.

"Pip," he said gently, "it's time for breakfast."

Pippa made a quick move out from between Rick's legs, went around the outside of the sheets, and stopped on top of his head, snuggling and pushing downward until he had wedged himself between his shoulders and the pillow.

"Well, alright! Let's go eat, buddy."

Pippa jumped off the bed in one motion and was already waiting at the kitchen counter jumping on his hind legs when Rick caught up with him.

"I see you. Let me get it together."

Pippa was usually very content once he'd eaten and would curl up on the couch while Rick drank his coffee. This time he wanted to go for a walk right away, and he was standing at the top of the staircase whining and grumbling until he was sure that Rick was putting on his shirt and pants. For once, he sat at the top of the stairs calmly waiting for his harness.

"I guess you really want to go for a walk?"

Pippa bounded down the stairs, and Rick followed behind less enthusiastically. When he opened the outside door, there was a rush of warm air, and he had to pull the leash to keep Pippa from running into the street.

There was always one day that Rick first noticed springtime. He had taken note of it every year since he was a teenager. It was the day that girls started wearing short skirts. The warm air seemed to circulate up, under, and around them to invigorate Rick's olfactory system. Birds chirped louder. It was unmistakable. Now the first sign of spring was a shorter version of the skin-tight exercise pants that women wore all winter.

"We're witnessing the death of femininity, Pip. Look at these women. They're all going to spin class, or yoga, or they're not going to exercise at all. Either way, what should be enticing is just wrapped up in plastic-looking material."

Pippa looked up and panted happily as he was talking and then went back to sniffing the sidewalk. Rick knew it was a bad sign that he was so focused on what these 20-something women were wearing. They were out of his league, at least in terms of their generational differences. He may as well have been "Dad" to them, and now he had started to act like it.

This realization brought back a nearly 10-year-old memory from a night at a bar in New Jersey. He had been ready to settle down on the couch when he decided he was failing as a single man if he wasn't out on a Friday and said to himself, "I have to go have a beer and give it a shot. See some people. Give myself a chance, at least."

He walked to a nearby spot and found a seat around the back side of the crowded U-shaped bar giving him a view of almost everyone there. Each person seemed to be in a group or paired up with someone else. Instead of a pick-up spot, this felt like he'd crashed someone else's party. He was the stranger watching other people's lives. As he was taking his last sip of beer and getting ready to leave, two very attractive, and very young, women came around the bar and sat next to him, even though there were several open stools on either side. They seemed under 21, and the candy cane that one of them was sucking made her look even younger. They each ordered a light beer, and Rick signaled the bartender for another one without acknowledging them. One of them was wearing so much perfume that his eyes were watering, but he didn't care.

After they finished, he thought better of it for a moment but then blurted out, "Can I buy you ladies a beer?"

It sounded more creepy coming out of his mouth than it did when he'd decided to say it, and candy-cane girl replied, "No, thank you. We're leaving," as she poked her friend in the arm.

"OK. Have a good night," he said feeling embarrassment wash over him as he stared down at his hands folded on the bar.

As they got off of their stools to leave he heard the other woman say, "Why are we leaving!? He was cute."

Candy-cane girl shot back, "Are you kidding me? He's as old as your uncle!"

That was the moment Rick realized that the life he thought he would live had already happened. It passed by before he realized it. He had a chance to live it but squandered it. He was still cute, but he was now the avuncular form; not sexy and not cool, just reminiscent of some young, candy-cane sucking, overly perfumed woman's friend's uncle.

People always stared and smiled at Pippa when they walked down the street. Rick had become accustomed to it, but the dog was adorable, and it couldn't be denied. Pippa was a magnet for young, female college students in particular, and a small group of them were approaching on Fifth Ave. The dog was expert at this, spotting them visually first before starting to pull toward the group, body low-slung, crawling along in supplication. Once the aural cues began, with the young women emitting high-pitched "oohs" and "awwws," Pippa would go into overdrive, sealing the deal by rolling over on his back exposing his pink belly to their pats and rubs. This, of course, increased the excitement for both Pippa and the young women until it reached its natural crescendo resulting in an unexpected fountain of urine on one of their feet. Everyone was usually smiling and thankful for the quick break in the day despite the pee, so Rick allowed this cycle to continue as a general public service.

"If there's one thing I have going for me, it's this dog," Rick thought. "He knows how to work the room. I just need the right room."

They continued walking into Washington Square Park, and Pippa pulled him along with uncharacteristic abandon. Rick had recently ordered a shoulder bag with a harness to carry Pippa, but they hadn't christened it yet.

"We're going on an adventure, Pip. You will be my Watson and come along with me as I look into this Ridley mystery."

Pippa looked up and wagged his tail then went back to sniffing the sidewalk.

The Metropolitan Transportation Authority's rules of conduct state that any pet may be brought on a train or bus as long as it is "enclosed in a container and carried in a manner which would not annoy other passengers." Of course, this rule has invited many creative workarounds including bags with leg holes for larger dogs. Rick had seen a lot of bad things on the subway over the years, and animals were never the problem. Even the rats normally kept to themselves. He thought Pippa would be OK inside the bag, since Claire had told him she carried him around in her purse for a year when he was a puppy. She tried to pass him off as a support animal of some kind, but the barking and whining didn't go over very well in restaurants and movie theaters. Rick knew some would think he was one of those people now that he had the bag, but he didn't care. He had bought it with the dog in mind rather than his own comfort and thought it would be good for Pippa to go further afield and see some new sights. He didn't ask for a dog in his life, and he didn't want to believe that he needed the dog. Of course, they both needed each other, but this was a fact only Pippa knew at that point.

After looping back around, they arrived at the townhouse as a couple was parallel parking in front. Pippa lingered at the first step giving the woman his best look of desperation as he rolled onto his back. The usual script played out, and the man just missed a spray on his shoe.

As they were walking away, Rick heard the woman say, "I wonder who he is?"

"Just somebody's dog walker," her companion responded.

Rick chuckled as he entered the foyer and pulled off Pippa's harness. He had heard this before when walking him during the work day. One pair of young students once surmised, a little too loudly, that he was either a dog walker or "some old queen's boy toy."

"Yup. That's what I am for sure, Pip. I'm somebody's dog walker alright, and that somebody is you!"

He made a quick move toward the stairs as if to race, and Pippa ran past him and turned to face him at the top barking in staccato once he realized he'd been duped. Rick followed him slowly feeling an ache in his knees. About a third of the way up he grabbed the railing for support as his right one buckled just in time to hear the usual creaking squeak on that single stair tread.

"This time it's mocking me," he grumbled.

He made himself a cup of coffee, grabbed an apple and banana off of the kitchen counter, and went up to the secret room to continue the research. He sat in front of the monitors and looked over his shoulder at the row of fake books wondering how he could have missed this obvious mismatch with Ian's personality. He opened Adam Smith's *Wealth of Nations* and found a square plastic box with a label that resembled a symbol on the periodic table of elements. It said, "Gth" and "Ghost Train Haze" in smaller type.

"This seems like an appropriate aid to my investigation," he said.

He wasn't sure where this was going yet, but tomorrow's weather looked good for a walk to the scene of the crime.

Chapter 12

Pippa stood stiffly at the foot of the bed staring at the tree outside the window and barked incessantly at a chirping bird, so all hope of sleeping a little longer was lost. He tried to ignore the racket and pretended to be asleep when Pippa came bounding over to sniff his ear. There was no hope. It was Saturday morning at 6:30 a.m., and it was time for the two of them to start the day. Rick began the belly rubs to calm him down as he quickly mapped out the walk to Allen St. in his mind and tried to wake up.

After he'd sampled the Ghost Train Haze the day before, Rick was keenly focused on the task and stayed there all day writing, researching, and scrawling quick notes on people who might have been involved. He walked Pippa once more after dinner but found himself back in front of the monitors until nearly midnight to dig a little deeper on the years after the brothers sold the company assets. There wasn't much information available.

There was a wealth of one-column newspaper advertisements to review and also a few glowing editorial pieces that laid praise on the store's offerings, recounting the throngs that descended in waves upon the various departments for the spring sales. These articles sounded a lot like the thinly veiled advertising Rick had written during his career.

The ads didn't tell him anything he didn't already know. It was notable that Ridley & Sons kept using "Cheap Store" as their sub-headline until just after the founder died unexpectedly in 1885. There was a short period of growth, and the complex of buildings that housed the various departments was made more unified. Business continued on for another 15 years, and then the two brothers liquidated the assets. After this, all that he could find was a legal notice published in *The Brooklyn Eagle* showing the conveyance of Ridley & Sons properties to Edward, Jr. in 1902, and then a little later there were a couple of notices of Ridley's foreclosure on properties in Manhattan and The Bronx. There seemed to be a lot missing in between, and he was still wondering how Ridley found his way out to Fanwood, NJ and what happened for the 30 or so years he lived there before the series of brutal murders in the damp sub-cellar below 63 Allen Street.

Pippa was laying on top of his head now, and Rick picked him off gingerly so that he could sit up and get out of bed.

"Alright, you asked for it, Pip. We're going to eat something and hit the road. You're going in this bag," Rick said as he produced it from a box under the kitchen counter. Pippa looked suspiciously at the strap and growled.

There was a quick practice run around the kitchen and some small adjustments to the strap to make it more comfortable on Rick's shoulder, and the two set off. His plan was to walk as normal heading south through the park and then put Pippa in the bag whenever he got tired or stopped walking altogether. The sky was perfectly blue, undulating in stark relief as it dipped in between the buildings now and then. He was proud of Pippa. They had walked all the way to Spring St. before he looked up stubbornly and sat down. He pulled a portable dog bowl from his backpack and filled it.

"Hmmm, maybe not the best idea to give you a lot of water before I carry you in this bag, huh?"

Pippa let out a few squeaks and jumped in as the bag was lowered to the sidewalk. He nestled into it and poked his head over the top as they continued to walk.

"OK, fellow investigator and passenger, we're closing in on the scene of the crime. Not too much further now."

It was still very early, and the streets were mostly empty except for a smattering of dog walkers and joggers. They were covering a lot of ground now that Pippa wasn't stopping to smell everything, and it wasn't long before they'd crossed through SoHo and into the Lower East Side. Rick stood at the corner of Allen and Grand and looked up. If he didn't know what he was looking at, he couldn't have pictured the huge presence Ridley & Sons had on these blocks. Almost half of the original storefront portion of the buildings had been shaved off when the city widened Allen St. in the late 1920s.

As a result of the widening, it was difficult to picture the grand entrance on the corner and the domed roof with Ridley's triangular pennant flying above the track level of the elevated train. Rick had found a mention of "Ridley's Stop" on the El which meant disembarking at the corner of Grand and Allen. He had studied the illustrations and old photos and it was still difficult to picture what was once here. He tried to imagine those throngs of customers rushing through the front doors in what was now the northbound lane of Allen St.

"It's no wonder people don't care about the past," Rick thought. "It's hidden all around us, and it's too much trouble to go looking for it."

Pippa had snuggled himself into the bottom of the bag and started to make his contented sounds. It was close to a whine but sounded more like a sigh, and he poked his head and paws over the top panting happily. Rick turned to look across to the garage at 63 Allen St. and saw the sun blaze into the bottoms of the dull windows on the second floor as it crested the rooflines on the east side of the street. His instinct was to take a picture of the garage and the dog in that order, but he did neither and just stood there taking in the moment.

The building had originally been a stable for the nearby church, and Ridley had purchased it when the wholesale delivery business became so brisk they needed a convenient place to house the fleet of wagons and teams of horses. The space was converted to a garage as many others had been by 1920 in the city, and Ridley insisted the unusual sub-cellar be renovated for use as his personal office. The building already had several shallow ramps that had led down to the former stables, and his office was connected to that by a short flight of stairs. This lowest level consisted of two distinct areas: an ante-room next to the staircase that served as the entryway; and another larger room with Ridley's desk near the door and his secretary's toward the rear.

Rick walked over to the unmarked door to the right of the entrance and thought about turning the knob. There were also two doors labeled "UP" and "DOWN" to the left of the garage entrance. The illustration in the article he'd seen from 1933 indicated that the private basement entrance was to the right of the main entryway. This would seem to make sense, since the two separate street-side doors to the left indicated both up and down, and the only way to Ridley's office was down. Rick stood in front of the door and wondered if he could just will himself through it; turn the knob backward in time, and just walk down the horse ramps to descend the lower stairs. He could feel himself on the same path that Ridley took.

The garage was open 24 hours, but there wasn't anyone to speak with about a quick visit to the sub-cellar. There was a young man inside a glass-windowed booth at the main entry who said he was only there to take a ticket, call for the car, and ring up the payment.

"I don't get paid to give tours. Just get cars up here and get money from people before they leave," he said quickly.

"OK. I couldn't give you a small parking payment in exchange for an unescorted walk through that door out there? We could pretend I'm a car parking for about an hour. How much would that be worth to you normally? I won't even ask you to see me out when I'm done. I'll just find my own way and say goodbye. I'm an easy customer. Just doing some research. No trouble," Rick shot back.

The parking attendant looked back and forth between Pippa, who was panting eagerly half out of the bag, and Rick, who was trying to look professional.

"OK. What does it matter? Nothing down there. I've been down there," he said.

"Oh, you've been in the sub-cellar?"

Rick said this with surprise as if he must have seen something very interesting down there.

"Nah, yeah, I guess. I went down there a few times. The boss has some stuff stored down below. You like paper towels?"

Rick laughed. "Yes, I hate to admit that I use paper towels."

"Well, that's what was down there last time I looked. Some cleaning stuff. You doing research on cleaning?"

"In some ways I guess I am," Rick said without smiling. "What's your name?"

"It's Hyung," he said as he rolled his eyes and looked down at the time-stamp machine.

"Did you ever want to solve a mystery, Hyung? When you were a kid, did you ever want to dig until you reached China?"

Hyung looked up at Rick angrily and said, "I'm Korean."

"That was a bad analogy. I meant did you ever dig a hole and find something that amazed you as if it were there waiting for you to find it. Did you ever wonder what's right below your feet as you walk?"

"I usually just watch out for dog shit when I walk," Hyung said through clenched teeth as he stared through the glass at Pippa.

"OK, so we're not off to a great start here," Rick said mildly. "What can we do to make this thing happen? I just want to take a walk downstairs."

"You can go fuck off," Hyung screamed suddenly.

"OK. That sounds like you're saying we don't have a deal here," Rick said.

"That's right, asshole. Get out of here now. You and your little stupid dog."

"OK, OK," Rick said as he moved toward the street. "You do know that I will never park my car here. I won't stand for this type of treatment."

"Screw you, your dog, and your car, too, asshole," Hyung yelled.

Rick walked to the far side of the garage where there appeared to be another side door on the satellite view he'd seen. It was hard to tell if it was an entrance to the crime scene or just another access door. Pippa started to whine and scratch at the top of the bag, so Rick hooked the leash into his harness and let him down. He promptly walked over to the entrance of the garage and lifted his leg. Rick thought this was an appropriate response to Hyung's unkindness when the silence was broken by a female voice.

"Oh, my god, a little Doxie! He's so cute! I love him! Could I pet him? I have one at home."

She spoke quickly, and there was an exuberance about her. She was still breathing heavily, slightly running in place, and her curly, brown hair was pulled into a pony tail and swung side to side hypnotically as she shifted from foot to foot.

"Hi, thanks. Good morning," Rick said nervously. "You have one of these crazy pups, huh?"

"Oh, yes," she said smiling radiantly, "I have my little girl Charlie."

She knelt down on the sidewalk to pet Pippa, and he immediately rolled over on his back for a belly rub, his mouth open and panting. He was in heaven, and she was having a similar effect on Rick. He couldn't remember the last time he felt this way when a woman smiled at him. He didn't want to give in to those old feelings, but he also didn't want them to stop. He was watching her with Pippa and felt himself smiling widely unable to say anything. It was a moment of purity, and nothing needed to be uttered to fill in the space between the two of them.

"What a cute little boy. Oh my god, I want to steal you. I want to bring you home with me," she said in a babyish voice that was not the least bit annoying.

Rick finally forced himself to stop grinning like a fool. "You have a girl named Charlie, and I have a boy named Pippa. That's cute," he said softly.

She looked at him and twisted up her face. "Pippa? I thought I gave my dog a gender inappropriate name," she said giggling. "I'm Cille, by the way. Like short for Lucille."

"I'm Rick," he stuttered out.

"People always get confused with my name," she said, "but I never liked Lucille very much, and I definitely didn't want to be called Lucy."

"I think that would have been too much for me this morning. Ricky meets Lucy," he laughed.

Pippa started his "hey, hey, hey" whining as soon as she turned her attention away from the belly rubbing and stood up to face Rick.

She was still out of breath with a slight glow of perspiration, and he thought she was the most beautiful woman he had ever seen. A small breeze picked up, and Rick felt slightly dizzy when he caught a hint of her scent. The sun was higher now over the tops of the buildings around them making her look almost ethereal. They were standing on a sidewalk outside of a dirty old garage with car exhaust hanging on the air, but Rick could only see and smell Cille. It was an essence. He had heard people talk about auras, and she had one.

"Do you go by Ricky?" Cille was smiling widely and looking at him intently now.

"I do not. The adult version of me doesn't go by that at least. My family used to call me that when I was a kid. I'm a Richard but I didn't like that, or Rich, or Dick…so Rick it was!"

"Well, pleased to meet you, Rick," Cille said as she stood up straighter and thrust out her hand.

Rick took her hand and shook it very slowly.

"Now, this is where you say, 'It's nice to meet you, Cille' or something like that," she said with a laugh.

"I'm sorry," he said snapping to attention. "I'm a little awkward sometimes. I'll warm up right after we part company, I'm sure."

Cille laughed, and he felt his face flush. It wasn't embarrassment but a feeling of calm and comfort while she chuckled. It was a real laugh, and it washed over him. Pippa was having a tantrum trying to get their attention, so Rick scooped him up and put him back in the bag.

"Nice ride, Pippa," she said as she patted him on the head. "So, what are you two doing here? You guys live around here?"

"No, we took a little stroll this morning. I carried him halfway. We're living at a friend's place on 12th St. between Fifth and Sixth."

"Oh, wow. I live near Stuytown on 15th. That's funny. So I guess I should wonder what we both are doing here this morning. I normally don't run this way, usually along the river, but I felt like taking a new route. I just decided to run wherever the mood took me today."

"My trip was planned," he said. "We came to this particular spot for some research on something I'm writing, and this is my little Dr. Watson."

"Interesting! What did you two find out?"

"Well today I found out that the parking attendant doesn't like me or my 'stupid little dog,' so I didn't get very far. There were unsolved murders in the basement of this garage. I just wanted to get a look at it."

Cille looked slightly shocked.

"I know, that sounds weird. I'm really not weird, I promise. The murders happened in the 30s."

Rick realized that this denial also sounded weird and changed the subject.

"Would it be too forward of me to ask for your number? Maybe we could meet somewhere else on purpose next time? Perhaps a play date with the two pups?"

Cille blushed and smiled so sweetly that Rick felt like he couldn't breathe.

"Of course!" Cille said, "That would be great. I'm not exactly at my best right now. I promise I'll shower before we meet next time." She reached out and touched his hand. "Give me your phone."

Rick handed her his phone, and she quickly added her name and phone number.

"Here you go, Rick."

He looked down and saw she'd used the puppy icon next to her name.

"Here, you give me yours," she said handing him her phone.

Rick couldn't think of anything cute, so he just added his name, phone number, and email.

"Well, Mr. Rick Gordon," Cille said as she took her phone back, "when may I expect your call?"

Rick looked down at his phone again. "It won't be long, Ms. Cille Golding. It won't be too long."

"Well, OK! Talk soon then. Bye, Pippa!"

He stood staring as she started jogging north on Allen St. past the Chinese shops across Grand St., and he kept standing there until he couldn't see her anymore.

"What just happened, Pip?"

Pippa let out a long sigh as if on cue and snuggled his head against Rick's chest.

"I agree. She's really something. OK, let's go home."

They walked west and meandered north to Sullivan St. and on to Washington Square. It was already 9 a.m, and the park was bustling. He took Pippa out of the bag and put him down once they'd passed the "Large Dog Run" that never failed to traumatize him. He seemed more relaxed than usual with all of the people and other dogs surrounding him, and Rick felt completely at ease, too. He stopped and sat on the edge of the fountain with Pippa on his lap and looked at Cille's name and little dog icon on his phone. He held his breath as he touched her number and the call connected.

Cille had probably just gotten home and answered breathlessly, "Hello, Rick! That was fast."

"Hello, Cille. What are you doing for dinner tonight?"

There was a brief pause, and he felt blood rushing to his face.

"That would be great," she said. "What time? Where do you want to meet?"

She was saying "yes," and Rick hadn't thought about the next part.

"Good question," he said laughing nervously. "How about 6?"

"Perfect," she said with excitement. "Do you want to meet sort of half-way? There's a good place on 13th and Third called Donnelly's. Sound OK?"

"Yes, see you then!"

He put his phone in his pocket and smiled down at Pippa who looked back up at him panting happily.

"I know, Pip. I feel the same way. Let's go home before something happens to screw this up."

Chapter 13

Rick put on the jeans and white shirt combination that had worked so well on his last date and paced around for a bit. It was only 4:45. He took Pippa around the block, and it was still only 5:15. He thought about paying a visit to the secret room, but he didn't want to get sucked in with research or Ian's stash and make himself any crazier than he already felt. He decided to start walking very slowly.

He paused halfway down the stoop to look at the building diagonally across the street. It always interested him because of its oddly shaped east side that jutted out at an angle with the building next to it recessed behind it. It looked older than the buildings around it. He crossed the street and checked the address on his phone. To his surprise, the story behind the building popped up right away. It had been built in 1846 along the Minetta Creek, and the angled wall had butted up against the stream bank. In fact, the whole building was tapered into a triangle to allow the water to pass. He had noticed part of the creek flowed right under 12th St. when he'd looked at the old maps and wondered where it went. Once the Minetta was forced further underground, the building to the east of it was built over the former watercourse in 1868.

Rick wondered about the original owner's choice of location directly up against the flowing water, since there would have been other lots available on the new street at the time but then thought perhaps it was considered prudent to have a supply of fresh water. This branch of the creek was fed by a spring near the corner of Sixth Ave. and 16th St. After the Croton Distributing Reservoir was completed 30 or so blocks uptown, New Yorkers began dumping refuse into it around the same time that the house was constructed. This new supply of fresh water from upstate, this monumental feat of human engineering, had made the meandering Minetta Creek an inconvenient, unsightly, and unhealthy mess. Most of all it stood in the way of progress. The eastern branch wound its way from the vicinity of 21st between Fifth Ave. and Broadway like the prehensile tail of the Flatiron Building that would emerge many years later.

Both branches joined together to continue in a southwesterly direction toward the Hudson River.

According to the 1865 *Sanitary & Topographical Map of the City and Island of New York* drawn by Egbert Ludovicus Viele, the era's expert on the city's original topography and waterways, that convergence appeared to be directly underneath Ian's townhouse.

He took a picture of the angled wall and looked back across at the townhouse imagining the streetscape as it might have been in 1846. When he looked down at his phone again he realized he'd now need to rush to get to the restaurant on time.

Donnelly's was the kind of place he knew well: long bar, wood paneling, the hint of soured beer in the air. He was at home here. He'd always gravitated to more sophisticated places for first dates just to make the subtle point that he wasn't a drunken barfly, and that he had some class, but this place was perfect. He saw her standing by the bar. She was smiling at him, and he realized he would be happy if they were meeting at a hot dog cart in Times Square.

"Hi! You look beautiful," Rick gushed.

"Aww, you're sweet. I told you I was going to shower and everything," she said batting her eyes dramatically with one hand on her hip and the other fluffing up her hair.

She was doing her best Mae West, and Rick was smiling so widely his face was starting to hurt. Cille had her long, curly hair pulled back loosely so that some of the pieces had fallen to frame her face. Even in the dim light of this Irish bar she looked like an angel to Rick.

"Well, I can confirm that whatever you did has worked. Although I thought you were pretty damn beautiful this morning, too."

"You were pretty hot yourself with that little doxie peeing on the wall of that dirty garage," Cille said as she playfully jabbed him in the arm. "Want to get a table?"

They sat in a small, two-person booth across from the bar. The place was starting to get crowded, but Cille and Rick didn't notice. Because of the cramped space, they touched knees and feet accidentally as they sat. The two were giddy, and they'd only had one drink. The conversation came easily, and Rick resisted the urge to talk too much. As he became more comfortable, he realized that he could say just about anything on his mind, and Cille wouldn't judge it. She put him at ease.

They talked about their careers, and she didn't seem concerned about Rick's self-imposed sabbatical or his dwindling prospects. Cille had been a graphic designer for clothing catalogs at several retailers in the city, and they shared stories about production snafus and crazy clients. She was leaving the following morning for a weeklong shoot, and he tried not to look disappointed. He didn't want to scare her off, but he knew he wanted to see her again as soon as possible.

"So tell me about the writing you're doing now," Cille said as she rested her chin in her linked fingers, her elbows on the table and her face almost close enough for Rick to lean in and kiss.

"It's sort of hard to describe," he started out, trying not to be distracted, "but it centers on a mystery. It revolves around the murders that happened in that garage, the ones I mentioned this morning that almost scared you away. There's a lot to it. It's intriguing, because there are unclear motives and three murders, and they were never solved. I'm writing it from the perspective of the main character who's trying to get to the bottom of it. It's going to be a fictional story around non-fictional events. I'm not even sure that makes sense to me let alone you or anyone else. It's the early stages. I'm getting excited about it, though."

"Well, that sounds like a good book and maybe a better movie. Is the main character you?"

She was looking deeply into Rick's eyes now and swirling her hair around her index finger.

"It's funny, I didn't think about it," he said uncomfortably. "He's probably a bit like me but maybe a little more self-destructive."

"Hmmm, yes, I see," she said raising an eyebrow.

"He hasn't had the same life experiences as me. He's much more virile and manly," he said with a laugh.

"Well, I think you're manly and virile the way you are, so your character must be some specimen," she said as she reached out and took his hand.

"I have an ongoing problem with being too nice," he said as he tried in vain to break her spell. "I don't think that, but women often tell me that."

"Well, I like a nice guy," she said without hesitation.

"Good, I didn't want to get tough on you, kiddo," he said in his best 30s movie gangster voice.

"So, that's how it's gonna be, huh?" Cille was playing along. "Well listen here, you mug. You'll be nice as long as I say you're nice, see?"

They both looked at each other, burst into loud laughter, and simultaneously looked around the bar self consciously. They were in sync.

They had already settled up and decided it was time to go after the waitress asked them if they needed anything else for the third time. They walked out together bumping into each other awkwardly once or twice as they negotiated the crowd around the bar and put their hands out to steady each other. Rick deeply inhaled her aroma again as her hair swung toward him. They stopped just outside the door and stood next to each other in front of the plate glass window. She took both his hands and started shaking them vigorously.

"It's the first date, right? We can't really officially kiss yet," she said nervously.

"Well not 'officially,' but we could try something simple and dignified, yet not quite official," Rick said. "Maybe a peck?"

"Sure," Cille said breathlessly as she leaned in.

Suddenly, Rick thought he was about to pass out. He put his arms around her shoulders and kissed her with a prolonged peck followed by a slight cheek kiss at which point his knees went weak as he inhaled deeply from the nape of her neck.

"That was nice," Cille whispered with her eyes half closed.

Rick didn't say anything. Instead he just looked at her wanting to remember the moment. He had a feeling this was it. Even though he'd had similar feelings with the wrong women several times before, it was nothing like this.

Rick smiled and said, "That was better than nice. When are you coming back again? Friday?"

"Thursday afternoon," Cille said. "Yeah, maybe we could have dinner again that night if I'm not too tired. Sound OK?"

Rick nodded yes, and leaned down again for one more quick peck on her cheek.

"Ooh, you just gave me goosebumps," Cille gushed.

"Me too, kid. Me too," Rick whispered in her ear.

They turned and walked in opposite directions, and he looked up at the moon low slung above the buildings. He thought he'd stop to call back for her or maybe take a picture and send it to cap off the evening, but nothing could have made the night any better. He wasn't even angry with himself for falling in love again at first sight. He was too old for that. He thought she might love him, too, but he didn't dare let himself get that far ahead. He wasn't going to screw this up.

Chapter 14

Rick was startled out of sleep at 5 a.m. Sunday morning. Pippa had plowed himself under the sheets all the way down to his feet as usual and wasn't budging. There was no audible sound that woke him. He heard himself gasping for air as he woke up, though, and it felt like he was momentarily stuck between a dream and reality. He was in between, and it was a feeling he'd experienced when he was younger. He had a dream when he was seven or eight that he'd taken his pillow downstairs and sat down at the piano. In the morning the pillow was missing but then discovered where he'd left it on the piano bench. Other times, in later years, he'd felt as if he'd leapt out of bed to run down the stairs or out of a hotel room reacting to some perceived threat. The sensation was realistic, and he often felt as if he needed to act quickly to fight off a feeling of dread.

He gently slid himself out from under the sheets, and Pippa didn't wake up. As he walked to the kitchen for a glass of water he realized he'd been having a dream. It came back to him quickly and vividly, so he searched for a pen and paper but couldn't find either. He took his phone and quickly typed out what he'd dreamed.

"Outside the garage on Allen St. Standing there with Pippa in the shoulder bag. It's nighttime. No one is around. The door opens, I walk through and turn right to walk down the ramp. Door closes and now it's dark except for a light at the bottom shining through an archway. Down to the bottom, around the corner to an open doorway with faint light shining from downstairs. Only a dim light like someone is holding a candle or there's a lamp behind a closed door. Pippa is whimpering and clawing to get out of bag. Bottom of the staircase now. Sickening thud, then a crumpling sound. Standing out of sight in the doorway. Pippa starts to bark. Gun shots. A woman screams, 'what was that?!'"

Rick stopped typing for the first time trying to remember what happened next.

"Maybe that's when I woke up gasping for air? That would be the most logical and most maddening place to wake up," Rick thought as he saw a message from Cille.

Thanks again for the pleasant company, laughs, goose bumps, etc. last night. At the airport early. Have a good day! Say hi to Pippa!!

Rick smiled, trying unsuccessfully to resist the urge to text her right back.

Can't wait for Pip and Charlie to meet!

Cille wrote back.

You're up early Mr. Gordon! :)

Haha, I guess I could sense you were about to contact me.

Well, I did have a great time last night!

Me, too!

I'm going to be busy this week but can't wait to see you on Thursday!

Yes! I'll find a place, or we can just go back to the last place. That worked out well.

Yes! It did. Then we'll organize that play date with the dogs. XO

XO

He put down his phone and stood in the kitchen staring at the coffee machine wondering if he should just give in and stay awake now rather than try to go back to sleep. He decided to spend as much of the day possible writing and working out his main character's back story. He'd never written anything like this before, and he had a sense that he was doing it all wrong, but he was happier than he'd ever been, and the day passed by quickly.

He had the same dream that night and woke up before 6 a.m. gasping for air again. He couldn't make sense out of it, and some of the details that had seemed so vivid were just shadows once he was awake. He laid quietly with Pippa between his legs snoring and stared at the ceiling blankly. Remembering that Carolina would be coming later, he thought it would be good to get out for a while and avoid any more awkward moments.

He carried Pippa downstairs for breakfast and whispered, "Maybe this is a good day to take you back to Fanwood for a little vacation?"

Rick packed Pippa away in the bag, and they made the 7:32 train out of Penn Station arriving in Fanwood at 8:28 just in time to see the late commuters begin to gather for the eastbound 8:38. Although Rick had been fed up with the daily commute, he missed the odd comfort those scheduled times provided even if they were often incorrect. He also missed the sound of the wheels rolling along and the views out the window as the train crossed the Meadowlands, passed through the industrial areas around Newark, and continued along toward the familiar string of suburban towns along the Raritan Valley Line. As they passed through Cranford and approached Westfield he thought about Ridley who took the 8:18 each day according to the news accounts.

Leaving and returning on the same trains seven days a week, the conductors would have known him well. Everyone along his path to the office on Allen St. would have been familiar with the strange old man. His persistent presence had likely made him both notable and invisible. Had he become more ghost than man to the people who encountered him day after day? He had read about Ridley's Sunday habit of passing The Homestead boarding house upon his return and walking in a circle around the Episcopal Church about a quarter mile further up the road.

"That's something a ghost might do," Rick thought as he sat down on a bench in front of the old Fanwood station house. The family renting his house would be off to work and school already, but Rick called anyway to let them know he was stopping by to get his car out of the garage.

He heard his name being called and looked up to see Larry Bristol who had been friends with his Uncle Will. They volunteered with the local historical society before Uncle Will had gotten too sick to make it to the meetings. He had also become sick of the meetings, so the timing worked out well for him.

"How are you, Rick? It's good to see you buddy," Larry said.

"Hello, Larry! I'm good," Rick said with surprise. "Great to see you. I haven't been living in town lately. Me and this little guy just came in on the train about five minutes ago."

Pippa poked his head above the edge of the bag and barked three times followed by a high-pitched whine.

Larry laughed, rubbed Pippa under the chin and said, "Well, what are you two doing in town?"

"Just a little R&R," Rick said as he let Pippa out of the bag to greet Larry properly. "Actually, I'd love to take a look around the carriage house at some point. It might help with something I'm writing. Maybe you could show me around sometime if you still have the keys?"

"No problem," Larry said as he fished through his bag for a piece of paper. "My wife is home now if you want to stop over and get the key. I trust you won't do anything crazy in there," he chuckled as he looked over his glasses at Rick and Pippa. "Here's my address. I'll call June and let her know you're coming. Just drop it off in the mailbox when you're done."

Rick said, "Thanks," just as the approaching eastbound train's horn blew.

"I have to run and catch this," Larry yelled as the horn subsided. "Really great to see you, Rick. Give me a call or email me sometime. I want to hear about what you're writing."

"Will do. Thanks again, Larry!"

He waved as Larry rushed up the stairs to the south side of the tracks with his shoulder bag and rain coat trailing behind him.

The Bristols' house was between the station and the carriage house, so it was easier to stop there first before getting the car. The front door was slightly ajar when Rick and Pippa began walking up the long driveway. They lived on a rise that would have had a clear view of the train station when it was built, but now a thick growth of trees had created the kind of lush, suburban landscape the railroad's real estate company had promised. June was standing at an angle holding the storm door open slightly like a barrier as Rick and Pippa approached the front steps.

"Hi, Rick. I'm sorry, but I'm deathly allergic to dogs. Actually, as far as I know, any animal with fur will make me break out in hives. My throat closes up, you know?"

"Not to worry," he said jovially. "This little guy poking his head out of the bag here is a hypoallergenic breed." As the words came out of his mouth, he realized that assertion was probably false and continued, "Either way, we won't get too close just to be sure."

"OK. Here you go, Rick," she said as she held a tissue over her nose and mouth and dropped the keys into his hand. "You know, I was so sorry to hear about your Uncle Will. He was a very, very good man."

"Thanks very much for your kind words. He was a good man, that's for sure," he replied in a faraway voice as he gazed absently at the shrubbery wondering what else to say while Pippa started to squirm and whine in the bag perfectly on cue once again.

"Well, I better get this little bundle of allergens out of your way, June. Thanks for the keys. I'll just drop them later today in the mailbox and won't bother you again. Nice meeting you."

As Rick and Pippa turned to walk down the front steps, he heard the storm door close and then open again. He didn't look back until he heard June say, "Did Larry tell you about the pitch forks? Be careful of the farm tools, please!"

"OK, thank you," he said over his shoulder as they continued down the long drive.

When The Homestead was at its peak size at the turn of the century, it covered almost the entire width of a large lot that now housed the police station, municipal building, rescue squad, and fire house. The carriage house was situated off to the side and slightly behind it and was somehow preserved despite the demolition of the main home in the mid-1970s. Rick remembered his uncle telling him that there had been a lot of alterations made to the carriage house over the years, but there were also intact features in parts of the building. He approached from the direction the carriages would have entered on the Watson Rd. side and took Pippa off of the leash. He ran circles around Rick until they got to the door.

"Back in the bag, Pip!"

Pippa ran in one more tight circle and jumped deftly into the satchel. He was getting good at it.

Rick stepped into the main room and turned left to walk through a narrow hall with stables that had been left remarkably intact. There were leather harnesses hanging on hooks and bits of desiccated manure and hay on the old plank floors. A door straight ahead at the end of the hall had light streaming through its cracks. He had seen several old photos of the carriage house from this angle, and there would have been a low, rectangular wing through this door that probably housed equipment or perhaps a chicken coop. This had been the last property in town with a legal coop when the former mayor purchased it in 1936. Pippa poked his head up over the edge when Rick walked into the stalls and bent down to get a closer look at the manure. The dog sniffed the air as though he could sense the horses' presence and started a low growl that progressed into a squeak before he buried his head again.

Rick turned to the side where there was a door leading to open wooden stairs with a landing. It was the hayloft, and the dangerous farm implements that June Bristol had warned him about came into sight as he reached the top. There they were lined up across three dusty 2x6 planks on saw horses facing the staircase like silent sentries guarding an old secret. Despite many years of oxidation, the tines on the pitch forks were still extremely sharp. It was as if they had been put away one last time when there was no more hay to bail and never touched again. The original pulley was in place, and the hay door was just slightly ajar. Iron grates along the lower wall and floor allowed the feed to be shuttled down to the stables. It was easy to imagine this as a working barn housing the horses, carriages, and sleighs. One of the restored sleighs, with The Homestead painted across the side, was proudly displayed in front of the municipal building each winter.

He looked out the window in the direction of the old boarding house and tried to picture the scene around 1900. There were no cars, and the world naturally ran at a slower pace. The train was remarkably fast in relation to any other form of conveyance, and it hadn't gotten much faster over the years. Rick had looked at some of the old train schedules, and it amused him that it was just over an hour to downtown Manhattan in 1868 even though it involved switching to the ferry at Elizabeth. Later the train went to Jersey City, and commuters boarded a ferry there. Then the train tunnels under the Hudson River were built, and the line was routed through Newark. It still takes a little more than an hour door to door 150 years later if all goes well.

"Ridley would have walked out through the front, I'd guess, and then turn right down the sidewalk on Martine Ave. to the station," Rick thought. "Or would he have the habit of walking this way toward Russell Rd.?"

He walked to the other side where they'd entered the building and looked down from the window.

"I'll bet he took the higher ground given his penchant for galoshes and overcoats," Rick said. "He walked in and out of the front door every day."

Pippa was starting to squirm, so Rick took him downstairs, locked the door, and walked him down to the street.

"Well, do you want to go for a hike? We're going to get the car and go to your favorite place."

Pippa began to run in tight circles twisting the leash around his legs. Rick was nearly jogging to keep up, and he pulled him even harder when they got closer to the house. It was a short drive to the Watchung Reservation, but Rick was enjoying being behind the wheel again. He usually traced the same route through the old deserted mill village, past a revolutionary-era graveyard, along the Blue Brook, and around Lake Surprise. He felt at ease on the trails here. Pippa was not a long-distance hiker, but he always loved coming here and had already covered several miles without hitching a ride in the bag. They'd come to the crest of a long hill, and Pippa knew going down meant climbing back up the other way, so he dug in and sat down looking around anxiously with his nose turning from side to side in the breeze.

"Alright, let's head back now, Pip."

As they turned onto the path leading toward the parking lot, Rick heard a voice in the distance yelling, "Good one, Johnny!"

He stood there for a moment holding Pippa back waiting to hear something else, but there was only the sound of birds chirping. He hadn't thought about his father in a long time, but the voice sounded just like him. He was a soft-spoken man, but he had always been excited for his son's small accomplishments. Rick had heard this voice when he learned to ride a bike on his own, when he threw a strike in little league, or sank a long putt on the golf course. His father had been there to punctuate those moments with a cheer just like that one. It was the sound of pride. It had been more than 30 years since he'd heard it, but sometimes he could swear his father's voice was on the wind saying, "Good one, Ricky!"

It made him smile even though he was still sad to think about his mother and father after all of these years. He remembered being upset with them before they'd left for dinner that night. Chrissy, the babysitter, was upstairs saying goodbye to them, and he stayed down in the basement watching TV as they pulled out of the driveway for the last time. He always wished he'd run upstairs to give them a hug or at least tell them he loved them. It didn't matter now, of course, but he had always been determined to hold onto the memory of his parents and not let them fade away forever the way they seemed to on that summer night.

Pippa was running ahead happily now as he realized they were heading in the proper direction. Rick trailed behind still trying to hear that voice on the wind. He was crying, and he wasn't sure whether the tears were for himself or his poor parents. They had no way of knowing they'd just had their last supper when they were hit by the truck on the Garden State Parkway that night, and Rick had no idea he was about to become an orphan. Luckily his Uncle Will was there, and he became like a father to him. They both shared the loss together, and that made it easier even though things were never the same.

The sun was streaming through the thick growth of trees projecting bright, shifting patterns on the dusty path as they walked toward the parking lot. Pippa stopped running and looked back at Rick with his tongue hanging out, and suddenly all of the sadness washed away. Things were good. He thought about Cille and smiled even wider.

"What the hell do I have to cry about, Pip?"

Pippa looked back as he said this and barked excitedly.

"You and I understand each other," he said as he leaned down to pat Pippa's head.

It was already lunchtime, so he stopped at the deli for a sandwich and went back to the house to drop off the car. Since the renters weren't home he opened the garage door and pulled out a chair so that he could sit and eat while Pippa explored his old back yard. He was happy rolling around in the grass and poking his nose under the shed and back porch. Rick noticed the box of old photos and files where he'd left it in the corner and pulled it closer. After carefully wiping his hands he took everything out of the box and laid it on his lap.

He wanted to be sure there wasn't anything else Uncle Will had left for him on Ridley. As he looked down at his feet he noticed one photo left in the box partially stuck under the bottom flap. He pulled it out and realized it was his mother's christening photo. He looked at the wryly happy expression on his grandparents' faces and the somewhat dour visages of his great grandmothers.

"People didn't smile for photos in the old days," he said to himself laughing.

He studied each of their faces and then his mother's. She was so small, swaddled in her dress, with much ahead in a life that would be cut too short. He expected to cry again but felt comfort and calm wash over him instead. He was the last in this line of Gordons. The rest of them were in a box one way or another. Some were buried nearby, and the remains of his parents and Uncle Will were carefully packed away in the garage. There had been a small memorial service for his father and mother at the time, but they'd had no final wishes or plans beyond cremation, so Uncle Will took the safe route and told Rick it would be up to him to take care of their remains as he saw fit once he turned 18. Then he told him the same thing 25 years later when it became clear that he wasn't going to survive the cancer. It had spread to the pancreas, and his doctor gave him less than a year.

Now it was just Rick, Pippa, and the three quiet charges. His parents' remains had become a sad and enduring reminder of their death because of his own inaction. When Uncle Will joined them Rick nestled the three boxes together between some lace tablecloths and napkins his grandmother had saved for special occasions.

"Some people put themselves in boxes even before they die," Rick thought.

He wasn't ready to pack it all up again and sat looking over each of the photos and papers one more time. He didn't want to say goodbye yet because it meant putting his family away again for a while. It meant nestling what was left of his past between the box of crystal glassware and his parents' wedding china. Now it was up to him as Uncle Will had said. He owed it to himself, and to everyone in the boxes, to take a shot at being truly happy for once. He knew the writing was something he had to do, but he wasn't holding out much hope that it would make any money. He also knew that he needed someone to love and who would love him. He could only work hard at writing and hope that he wouldn't lead himself down the wrong path again with the other.

"Love is like this Ridley thing," Rick thought. "I can't search for a solution to the unsolved murders of three men any more than I can go out and find love. Did I somehow stumble upon the latter accidentally while trying to do the former?"

He'd lost track of time again and didn't feel like rushing for the 2:35, which meant waiting nearly an hour before the next train out, so he decided to take Pippa for another walk around the neighborhood and stop in again at the carriage house before dropping off the key. It had gotten warmer, and there was a breeze blowing yellow-green tree pollen in visible swirls. Rick sneezed rapidly three times and put Pippa into the bag when they approached the door.

"Why am I going back inside? There's nothing here that can help me," he thought.

He walked up to the loft again to look out of the windows and tried to picture The Homestead and how it would have looked from behind. Martine Avenue was visible, and he realized that old Ridley would have disembarked around this time of day to walk this stretch of sidewalk with his bulky coat, galoshes, and umbrella; returning to The Homestead for an early dinner before the other boarders arrived to the dining room.

"Ridley really was living like a ghost," he thought. "It's not hard to disappear in New York City. Why did this rich man choose to live in a small town where he would stand out?"

Rick had been thinking about this a lot. Ridley's family had a large estate in Gravesend, but perhaps he wanted to distance himself from a half sister and the other relatives who lived there? Maybe he was attracted to the healthy aspects of the country? When Ridley first came to live in Fanwood around 1900 the city was a place of "bad air" during the summer. This could explain his choice of The Homestead, since it had been known as a bucolic retreat since the 1880s.

Rick's other theory had to do with Ridley's personal security. Living outside the city would have created a buffer from his tenants and other business associates. He imagined Ridley as a tough landlord who was quick to foreclose. Maybe it was hard for him to sleep at night knowing he'd made so many enemies, or he was afraid of robbery? Edward and Arthur had a younger brother James who was robbed and bludgeoned to death in 1874 on Canal St. shortly after leaving the store. It was said the thieves believed he was carrying a large amount of cash.

He narrowed his eyes as he looked toward the sidewalk thinking, "What if none of the murders was about money? What if it was all about revenge? It doesn't make as much sense, but maybe that's why the case went unsolved?"

No matter how much he turned it around in his head, there was no simple solution. This was not a logical thing. Rick had seen a few theories while he was doing research, and many of them were plausible. That was the problem. In the absence of solid evidence or a clear motive, and adding a little conjecture, anyone could have been the killer or killers. There were still too many variables.

"OK, Pip. Let's lock this place up," he said as he carefully edged past the rusted pitchfork tines and walked down the stairs.

There was no sign of June Bristol when he stopped to drop off the keys, but he thought he saw her pull back the living room curtain as he turned to walk down the driveway from the front walk.

"Nice but nervous," Rick thought.

The eastbound train would be arriving in 10 minutes, so Rick put Pippa down, and they walked quickly toward the station. Pippa seemed to like the train and fell asleep half out of the bag with his head resting on Rick's lap. He took out a pad of paper and turned it sideways. He wrote "Moench," "Ridley," and "Weinstein" across the middle, circled the names, and drew spokes around each.

"Where, when, and how do they intersect? That's the question," Rick thought.

He remembered the headline on one of the articles that announced, "It's not lack of clues but the abundance of them that baffles detectives…"

He looked down at Pippa lying at his side snoring. It had been a good day, and it didn't matter that he wasn't any closer to knowing where the story was going or how it might end.

Chapter 15

Rick was still carrying Pippa when they arrived at the townhouse. It wasn't the first time he felt like a father that day as he traveled with his companion in a papoose of sorts. People looked at him strangely, then they smiled and chuckled, and he couldn't blame them. He had become a "crazy dog person." There was no use in pulling back now and no way to alter this new path. Before he was a dog walker, but now he was a dog person with a helper animal.

"I still can't figure out whether I'm helping him or he's helping me," Rick thought as he laughed out loud.

He pushed open the door, and there was a dull clunk as if something heavy was dropped on the floor upstairs, and Pippa started struggling to get out of the bag. Rick knelt down to let him out, and he wriggled free running upstairs barking and growling as he went. He just assumed that Carolina was still upstairs and didn't rush to chase him, but the dog's barking became more frantic as he made it to the third floor, and then there was nothing. Pippa had gone silent. Rick ran up the next two flights, breathing heavily on the second one, and grabbed his bad knee for support until he saw Pippa's tail wagging back and forth at the top. He was on his back in belly rub mode.

Rick laughed breathlessly, "Enjoying yourself, little guy?"

Expecting Carolina to respond, he heard a low, menacing voice instead.

"Not as much as I am, old boy!"

Ian poked his head around the bannister and grabbed Rick by the neck.

"You scared the crap out of me," Rick yelled as he pushed his hand away. "I was expecting Carolina!"

"Disappointed are you?"

Ian pushed back at Rick, and he fell down onto the top stair tread.

"Not at all! Great to see you," Rick said as he picked himself up.

"I told you I'd be seeing you before long, mate," Ian boomed.

His years of traveling and living abroad had imprinted a melange of diction and dialect on Ian. He wasn't putting it on for show, or as an affectation, or a joke. He'd simply absorbed different ways of speaking and echoed them back to the people around him like a chameleon. He didn't have a choice, and he wasn't aware of it. That's what made Ian so successful.

"You are correct, my good man," Rick said as he smiled and hugged him around the shoulders. "I just didn't know it would be right now, here at the top of this staircase with you strangling me."

Ian was beaming with glee and bellowed, "Surprise!"

"You succeeded at that," Rick said as he stood to face him at the top of the stairs. "So how long are you here?"

"Believe it or not, mate, I'm probably leaving tomorrow. I needed to be in D.C. yesterday to testify. Don't ask! Done here already, and I need to get back in the next few days for some merger bullshit I'm dealing with now in Singapore," Ian trailed off as he walked toward the secret room. "Let's smoke a bowl and catch up a little. What do you say?"

"OK, sure. It would be validating to dip into the emergency supply along with its rightful owner. I've tried to moderate my usage," Rick said sheepishly as he followed him inside.

Ian quickly looked through the fake books on the wall. "Yes, I can see you've been quite judicious. I like that about you, my dear Richard. Waste not, want not."

Ian was the only one who could get away with calling him that. They had known each other so long that Rick knew he wasn't doing it to irritate him.

Ian ran his finger along the spines and stopped at *Moby-Dick*. "This should do the trick. Grape Ape is a nice, heavy indica," he said and then hollered, "Call me Ishmael!" as he opened the cover and pulled out the vial with a flourish.

They sat in the secret room talking for a couple of hours without realizing the passage of time. It had been like that since they were children. They could always say anything to each other without worrying about what the other would think. Ian was one of the few friends that remembered Rick's parents well. He lived down the street, and their mothers had been friends since they were babies. They were more like brothers, and it had become clear as the years passed that he was his only real friend besides Amanda.

"So let me get this straight," Ian said through squinted eyes. "You've been holed up in here researching an 85-year-old murder mystery for the last month, writing a book about it, and you also managed to fall in love again along the way?"

Rick fell back into the bean bag chair and Pippa ran up onto his chest.

"That pretty much sums it up," he laughed. "We've only been on one date, so I'm trying to 'take it slow' as they say. I've never met anyone like her, though. I worry I'm doing it to myself again, you know?"

"Yes, I do, but hey, man, you deserve to be happy," Ian said quickly. "I know you. Don't get yourself all bunched up and lovesick. Just enjoy life. Let it happen. Don't try to make it happen."

"That's very deep," Rick said in a mystical tone.

"I've been picking up a lot of eastern philosophy," Ian said bowing his head slowly with his hands in prayer position. "Want to get a beer and some dinner?"

"Sure, do you mind going downtown to pay our respects at The Green Door?"

"Ah, yes, let's go and see your buddy there," Ian said. "What's his name? Irv?"

"Close, it's Merv. Not sure he's working right now, but let's go anyway."

The sun was getting low, and the bar was dimly lit and about half full. A group of young guys in suits was clustered around the far corner talking and laughing loudly, and Merv was standing toward the back holding the remote control and glancing up at the television as if he hadn't moved since the last time Rick had been there.

"What do you say, Merv?"

"I didn't say anything yet," Merv retorted with mock anger as he turned his body slowly to face them. "Where the hell have you been, Rick?"

"I don't work around here anymore, Merv. It's a shame, I know. You remember my friend, Ian?"

"Of course, nice to see you again, Ian," Merv said cordially as he reached out to shake his hand.

There was a verbal crescendo punctuated by a group cheer from the guys in the corner for no apparent reason, and Merv twitched and shook his head.

"That lot is givin' me a headache," he said under his breath as he set down the glasses. "So, what are you doing with yourself now that you're not coming here every day? Where's work now that it's not around the corner?"

"Good question," Rick pondered. "I'm on my own for a bit."

"What do you mean by that? Single again? You told me about the Hoboken girl."

"Yes, do tell my good man," Ian said dramatically. "What is it that you're doing with yourself these days?"

"Well, I'll tell you Merv, I'm not sure what the hell I'm doing but it isn't work. At least I'm pretty sure it won't pay. I'm working on a book if you can believe that," Rick said dryly as he lifted his glass.

Merv said, "A book!" with a look of excitement Rick had never seen. "Did you get past the first page yet?"

Rick started to reply, but Merv cut him off as he turned his back and said, "Well, you're on the home road now."

Rick laughed as Merv walked toward the loud group and tilted his head back with a smile and a glint in his eye. This was his way of saying, "Good luck. Get to it."

Ian was quietly drinking his beer and smiling.

"You look good, man," Rick said.

"Thanks! I have a masseuse that's working out the years of knots. I feel better than ever. I get a head massage every day, too," Ian said as he pointed his ten fingers at his scalp.

"You have a good place?

"No, she lives in the house. It's easier that way. We spread it out. Not too much at a time," Ian said matter of factly.

"OK, that sounds pretty good, I guess," Rick said feigning boredom.

"I'm going to need to stay put for at least another year, so you're not only welcome to keep on living at the place here but you can also come and visit in Singapore. You look like you could use a daily head massage."

"Yes, you're correct. I could probably use one sometime this calendar year at least. What is it that you're doing there?"

Rick never pressed Ian for information about his business dealings, but he had been getting more curious lately.

"You know," Ian began slowly, "I have these companies. It's shoes these days. A lot of the manufacturing is happening in southeast Asia. I just need to be there to make sure all of the right decisions are made at the right time. I'm also still doing a lot of trading on the side…"

Ian went on for a few minutes without actually saying anything about what he was doing. Rick thought about asking him to see some photos of the shoes but stopped himself and thought, "Maybe he's the next mystery waiting to be unfolded if I ever finish this one?"

"OK. I get it. Sounds good," Rick said lying. "Seeing anyone over there?"

"Not really," Ian said as he tilted his glass all the way back.

Merv was there suddenly with two more beers and shots of whiskey before Ian could continue.

"So you boys getting up to some trouble? What's the occasion? Haven't seen this one around…"

There was another hoot and holler from the guys in the corner, and this time Merv wasn't having it and turned his attention to them.

"What d'ya think you're at a football match or something? Pipe down or move on. There are other places you might like. Have you been to that Chuck E. Cheeser's?"

Rick had to bite his lip as he always did when Merv chastised rowdy clientele. There was some grumbling in the group, and Ian got off of his stool, huddled them up together, and whispered something before continuing to the bathroom. They paid up quickly and left.

When he came back Rick asked, "What did you say to those guys?"

Ian settled into his stool with a big smile. "I told them me, you, and Merv here were going to kick their asses if they didn't leave by the time I got back."

Rick laughed, "More eastern philosophy?"

"Well, I figured they didn't want to get their suits all messed up. Even if they did get the better of us for some reason, they'd probably get bruised. They were pretty boys, and they didn't want that," Ian reasoned.

"Thanks for almost getting me into a fight," Rick said calmly as Merv poured another round of shots.

"I'd appreciate a vote of my own, if you don't mind, next time you want to start a brawl, pretty boys in suits or not," Merv deadpanned as he tilted back his whiskey.

There were some people at tables in the back room, but now the bar was empty except for the three of them. The sun was going down behind the palisades, and a golden light washed against the picture window.

"I wish you didn't have to head back right away," Rick said as he stared out the window. "I miss you, even though you try to get me killed."

"Well, there's no rush actually," Ian said with a glint in his eye as he half rose off of his stool and clapped him on the back.

"I thought you were heading back tomorrow?"

"I was thinking of making one small stop on the way. I have an investment to look over in Iceland. Need to see it and see the people up close, know what I mean? Want to come along?"

"No," Rick said quickly. "No. I don't think that's a good idea."

"Why not? You know you need a break from all of this…"

"That's a laugh," Rick broke in. "You talk as if I've been exiled here in New York against my will, put up in a small cell banging my cup against the bars. You've given me comfortable accommodations to say the least. I'm working on my own thing now."

"I'm just saying that you look like you could use a break," he said as he leaned in to whisper. "Before long you may just end up putting yourself in one of those tiny cells you talk about without even realizing it. Then it'll be too late, mate."

Rick took a long drink of beer.

"I don't think I'm quite that desperate, but thanks very much. Besides, I just met a great girl, and…"

"She sounds very nice," Ian interjected quickly, "but she's not here now, and, like you said, you just met her. Besides, what makes you think we're going to Iceland to get you laid? What, are you that vain? Are you that horny?"

Rick took a few breaths before responding, "You are always trying to get me laid. Why is that?"

Ian stood up indignantly, stopped, smiled, and then sat down.

"You're right. Strange. Why do I do that?"

"I have an idea," Rick said.

"What?"

"Remember Katie Beam?

Ian's face lit up. "Oh, yeah! She was such a cute girl. I haven't seen her since…"

"It was sixth grade," Rick interrupted angrily.

"Right. That's right. Sixth grade," Ian said with a wistful look in his eye.

"So, you remember what happened?"

Rick was staring at Ian now waiting for him to remember.

"Nope," Ian said shaking his head still smiling.

"It was the 'seven minutes in heaven,' you asshole."

"Oh, that! Oh. Sorry mate. Totally forgot."

"You knew I liked her, but you went in the closet with her anyway."

"Listen here, I didn't do anything in that seven minutes that any other 12-year-old boy wouldn't do in a dark closet. It wasn't much, I'll tell you that for sure. I do remember that you told me you liked her beforehand. It never would have worked out between you two, though. She became a cheerleader," Ian rationalized.

Merv came over and said, "What are you two bickering about over here? Are you planning your wedding or something? If it's a celebration, let's have a shot."

He set up three double glasses of mescal.

"Alright, forget Katie Beam. Forget it all. I'll go to Iceland with you," Rick said with a slight slur. "But I need to figure out Pip."

"Call Amanda," Ian said. "Isn't she preggers? Probably already barefoot and in the kitchen. She needs a pet."

"Oh, she would strangle you if she heard that. When are we leaving?"

"Tomorrow afternoon," Ian said looking down at his phone. "There's a flight at 2:10 out of JFK that gets us to Reykjavík by 11:40. We can stay over in the city that night and be on the road first thing Wednesday morning."

"How long have you been planning this, you crazy bastard?"

"Just for the last few minutes, mate!"

Rick tilted back his pint glass shaking his head while Ian rattled off additional details about the trip.

"Just leave everything to me, old salt. You find a home for your little dog for the next few days, and I'll take care of the rest."

Chapter 16

Rick hadn't been in touch with Amanda since her self-imposed pregnancy exile, so he wasn't sure how well this sudden Pippa-sitting request would be received. He texted her, found his small suitcase in the basement, and started throwing clothes on the bed that seemed to make sense for Iceland. Amanda replied almost immediately and said that he could bring Pippa over anytime in the morning. She had started working from home and was looking forward to having him around to keep her company.

He went to the secret room to gather up his handwritten notes and some of the news articles he'd printed out. He stood there holding them as if he were weighing them to test their veracity, balancing the papers on his hand in a futile effort to divine the truth. He thought about one of his high school history teachers who insisted students turn in a stack of note cards each week. He never looked at them carefully which led many of the students to stack the deck with older notes. One industrious classmate even glued several cards together to triple the volume. Rick thought this blind weighing of note cards was an analogy for something, but he could never quite decide what it was.

He fanned the pages out in his hands and sat down as he spread them across the top of the desk with a sigh. He wasn't going anywhere or even going to sleep until he tried to make more sense of the Ridley murders. He was starting to think he didn't have a story. Every theory was just a theory. Once he dove deep enough into the mystery, he found some had their own theories, and they covered practically every angle a writer could want to pursue. But Rick was seeking proof and the truth, and that was more foolhardy than seeking love. Neither was going to come to him just because he wanted it badly. He'd learned that much.

"Alright," he said under his breath as he started to move the notes into smaller piles. "I'm going to boil this down for myself. That's the only way I'll be able to move on with this."

He began typing out everything he knew in chronological order:

-Ridley and his brother liquidate store assets and go separate ways in 1901; Ridley moves to The Homestead, Fanwood, begins commuting to Allen St. at least six days a week for 30 years

-Longtime private secretary Herman Moench murdered in January 1931; he was shot twice; no apparent motive or robbery; Ridley discovers body after diverging from his usual schedule; provides no support for Moench's family

-Lee Weinstein, the brother of Harry, the garage manager, becomes new private secretary immediately after murder; he has no experience in accounting

-Weinstein conspires with George Goodman and Arthur J. Hoffman, accountants from The Bronx, to defraud Ridley of $210,000 by forging invoices for repairs and making payments to dummy companies beginning in September 1931

-Weinstein married under name of John Lee in Richmond, VA and living with his wife in midtown hotel; bought new car with check drawn on dummy company

-The conspirators also drew up a fake last will and testament naming Lee W. heir to $200,000 of the $4,000,000 estate with the understanding that Goodman and Hoffman would split one quarter of the inheritance for witnessing the document

-Weinstein shot seven times in May 1933 with same .32 revolver as Moench according to the police; gun never recovered; Ridley bludgeoned with metal stool; bodies found near door of office

-Police find secret room behind fake brick wall adjacent to Ridley's office; believed to be used by bootleggers as a cutting plant before the end of prohibition; not considered a factor by investigators

Rick read over the notes and thought, "So, what? What was the motive to kill Moench, and who did it? Was he mixed up with the bootleggers during the time that the cutting plant was active? Someone had to let them in and out with all of the bottles and the barrel or whatever held the undiluted moonshine. Was he also skimming from Ridley? Prohibition was in full swing in 1931 but nearly over by the time Weinstein and Ridley were killed. Could it have been the case that they knew too much about the bootleggers other 'operations' that were now going to be their main sources of income with the repeal of the 18th Amendment? Did Ridley kill Moench and hire Weinstein so that he'd keep quiet? Why would he kill Moench? And what does all of this matter now? Why would anyone care? Was it Weinstein's/Lee's wife trying to double cross him? Why did the killer need to shoot Weinstein seven times?"

Rick's eyes were watering, and he could hardly keep them open. He closed his laptop slowly and slid it into his backpack.

"Time to go to sleep, Pip," he whispered as he looked down and saw that the dog was already asleep by his feet. He carried him to bed, laid down next to him, and fell asleep in his clothes.

It was another fitful night with the same haunting dream that seemed to bear witness to the 1933 dual murder. He was standing just out of view on the stairs holding Pippa as usual. After the sickening sound of the body crumpling to the floor, Pippa barked, and an unseen woman screamed, "What was that!?" just before Rick woke up to the alarm.

They emerged from the bedroom at 6 a.m. as Ian was running up from the basement gym two stairs at a time with a towel around his neck. He paused at the top of the stairs, looked at Rick with narrowed eyes, and took a big swig of water before slapping him on the shoulder and saying, "Ready for the land of fire and ice, my viking brother?!"

Rick was still groggy and jumped a little when Ian screamed.

"My head is on fire, and I need ice for it. And coffee. That's all I've got right now. How are you so damn chipper?"

"It's the eastern way, grasshopper. Follow the path."

"Screw you and your path and your eastern way. Get lost," Rick grumbled as he pushed past him on the staircase heading toward the kitchen.

"You'll feel better if you drink the rest of that smoothie I made," Ian called down after him in a motherly tone.

Rick cringed when he heard this and started making a pot of coffee while he got Pippa's food together and gathered up enough supplies to cover him at Amanda's apartment for a few days.

He was looking forward to seeing her, but he was already reminding himself to keep it simple and not mention anything about meeting Cille. He hadn't thought about her much once Ian arrived, which he took as a sign that he wasn't getting wrapped up too fast. Then he looked down at his phone and noticed he'd missed a text from her the night before, and he had that usual feeling as his face flushed and his stomach got tight.

Hi, Rick! So busy this week. I can still hardly catch my breath at this altitude. How are you and Pippa doing?

He stood slightly hunched over looking at her text as he rubbed his eyes. His head was pounding, and it was two hours earlier in Park City, so he had some coffee, took a shower, and finished packing before replying.

Hi, Cille!

He paused briefly because he wasn't sure what he was going to say next.

I was wondering how you were doing in the mountains.

He stopped again and thought, "This sounds stilted and fake" and erased what he had typed.

Sorry I missed your text. I've been thinking about you up there in the high altitude.

He hit send and regretted it.

"Why can't I just tell her that I couldn't stop thinking about her until my old friend got here, and now I'm leaving for Iceland today because he wants me to get laid? That makes sense as a reply."

Cille was already typing.

Hi! Or HIGH! Yup, that's me. I've been at about 9,000 feet. I miss you, but I also miss oxygen. You're right up there.

He laughed but then hesitated trying to think of a something witty.

I miss you, too. You'll probably have superhuman powers when you get back to 10 feet above sea level! I'm going to Iceland this afternoon for a few days. Crazy.

Rick wondered what she was thinking. He also wondered what he was thinking.

My gosh! I'm so envious. I want to go someday. Wait, why are you going?

Rick didn't stop to think now.

My friend Ian is here, the one who owns the townhouse, and he cooked up this idea yesterday. Just a quick trip. I can explain…

Rick sent his reply as he thought, "Can I explain? I'm confused about this myself. I don't even know how long we're staying."

No explanation necessary! I want to hear everything about it. When will you be back?

This was a question he couldn't answer, and that drove Rick crazy. He thought, "Why do I get myself into these situations? Why do I just go along?"

And then he wrote back quickly.

Soon! Not exactly sure, but I plan to be home before the week is over. Are you free Saturday?

This deadline made Rick feel better about the trip. He felt as if he had taken some control, but he knew his destiny was partially in Ian's hands for the next few days. Things never changed. Ian always made the plan, and everyone else fell into line.

I will be free Saturday morning for our doggie play date and hopefully over the stress of the week, sleep and oxygen deprivation, etc. Looking forward to it. :)

He smiled as he took a sip of coffee, and Pippa started his low, grumbling whine that meant he wanted some attention.

"OK, Pip. We'll get ready and go for a little walk. Then you're going to spend some time with Auntie Amanda," he said soothingly as Pippa quickly flipped over for a belly rub.

He looked at her last message and decided it would be foolish to hold back.

I can't wait to see you! XOXO

He shook his head realizing he'd possibly executed the "XOXO" maneuver way too early in the relationship, and then she replied.

XOXO yourself, Mister.

Rick sighed with relief. "So far so good," he thought as another message arrived. It was a photo of Cille's dog Charlie wearing a t-shirt emblazoned with "Tough Bitch" in florid script.

Tell Pippa to get ready. This little girl's coming for him, and she means business ;)

Rick laughed and suddenly felt a lot better. She could make him feel like himself again from thousands of miles away. He replied with a photo of Pippa lying in his familiar prone position.

Oohh, that's enough to make Charlie blush. I have to get going for an early start. Don't forget to come back soon. XX

Rick sat looking at her message and thought, "I won't forget," just as Ian started yelling something incomprehensible down the staircase.

Rick stood up and Pippa followed him to the base of the stairs.

"What's that you say?"

There was a moment of silence, and then Ian's voice boomed loudly for effect, "I said, 'Be sure you pack hiking boots!'"

"Ah," Rick said mildly. "I packed them already."

"And waterproof pants. A jacket," Ian called down.

"OK, are we going on an expedition?

"Not really. It's the scout's rule. 'Always be prepared,' right?"

Ian came down to the kitchen and stopped yelling just before he said, "right?"

"Sure, it's my honor," Rick said under his breath.

"Feeling better now? You looked like death earlier," Ian said with concern and then mumbled, "don't forget to bring a bathing suit for the hot springs" as he turned on the blender to make another smoothie.

Rick shrugged his shoulders and hollered, "Yes, feeling better now," over the blender and then waited for it to stop before continuing. "I stayed up too late, and drinking with Merv on an empty stomach didn't help. I tossed in bed a little, had a terrible dream, but I'm fine now. Going to drop Pip off with Amanda in a bit, and I'll be back in time to leave for the airport."

"OK, mate. Don't be late," Ian said as he chugged back a bright-green concoction directly out of the blender pitcher. "We have a meeting with destiny. We'll be new vikings. Going down to do some boxing."

He threw quick jabs at the air as he ran back down the stairs, and Rick shook his head wondering what he was getting himself into with this trip. Ian's plans usually yielded a mix of happiness and pain, some good memories and some better not recalled. He gathered up all of Pippa's supplies and headed for the subway.

Amanda was in her pajamas when she answered the door with a perky, "Well, Mr. Gordon and his little sidekick Pippa!"

"Hi! You look comfortable," Rick said looking her over. "I've missed you and your laid-back pajama style."

"One of my favorite perks of working at home. I can be barefoot and pregnant but still large and in charge."

"Well, you wear it well, my dear. I miss you. Thank you for wrangling this little guy for a few days. I'll be back sometime Friday to get him."

"You mean you've actually been told that's when the trip is ending, or you are creating a self-imposed, need I say, spurious end date on your own, my dear?"

Amanda knew Ian well, and had slipped into lawyer mode.

"It's the latter," he said quietly hoping to downplay it and avoid the deposition. "It's when I'm coming home. I think he needs to head back to Singapore anyway."

"How did this little boondoggle crop up? Why is he even here? What's in Iceland, and why are you going there with him? I thought he would have been retired by now at the rate he was going," Amanda said in a rapid-fire manner.

"He seems to be doing pretty well for himself," Rick replied blandly with a shrug hoping to diffuse the line of questioning.

"Well, I'm happy for him and for you!"

That was it. Amanda turned and went into the kitchen, and Pippa was padding right behind her and jumping excitedly on the back of her thighs as she walked.

"I guess he'll be OK here with you," Rick said hopefully.

Amanda looked over her shoulder and winked.

"Of course, he will. I've entered into a mothering and nesting stage. He's safe with me. He might even want to stay when you come back to get him."

Amanda knew this would irritate Rick, but he didn't take the bait.

"I'm sure it'll be hard to tear him away from you. He'll be cleaving to you as I pull him from your grasp mercilessly when I return to take him back to his terrible life," he said sarcastically.

"We'll see," Amanda said in a singsong voice as she picked up Pippa and kissed him. "This little guy might not even remember you by the time you get back."

He leaned over to kiss them and said, "I can only hope he has that much fun. Thanks for taking care of him. I'm going to leave now to avoid the long goodbye."

"OK, Gordie. No worries! I'm a good mommy. I really am," Amanda said in her Shirley Temple voice.

"That's what I'm hoping," Rick said quietly. "I love you both. I mean all three of you. See you on Friday."

He turned to walk out of the apartment and heard Amanda say loudly in her "Good Ship Lollipop" stage whisper from behind the door, "Now that he's gone, we can have some real fun, right Pippa?"

Rick laughed under his breath and thought, "Not too much fun, please," as he hit the elevator button.

Ian was sitting in a chair in the corner of the parlor with his two bags laid neatly in the hallway by the front door when Rick returned. While he gave the overt impression that his life was chaotic yet effortless, he was meticulous about timing and preparedness and never left anything to chance. This is how he made it look so easy, but Rick knew him better than that.

"It's time to be vikings," Ian said stiffly. "Go grab your stuff. I have a car coming in seven minutes."

Chapter 17

Ian didn't relax until he was safely ensconced in his first-class seat. Rick sat down after stowing his bag, and the face he saw next to him had transformed into the normal Ian. On the way to the airport, through security, and while waiting to board, Ian was steel faced and focused. Now he was himself again or at least the self he normally presented to people around him. Rick realized he hadn't traveled with Ian since college.

"This is probably how it is with him now," he thought. "Maybe he's geared up because he's on a secret mission?"

He chuckled at this thought, and Ian flashed a look in his direction and asked, "What's so funny?"

Suddenly he realized that Ian was self-conscious, and it was the first time he had ever seen that side of him. He was always the slick one. He always came off as the suavest guy in the room no matter where he went. Rick didn't know why it never occurred to him that Ian was just a regular guy who was very good at appearing confident. It was his parlor trick, his number one job skill, and it had served him very well.

"Nothing, man," Rick said calmly. "You good?"

"Who me? I was born good, mate," he said with a snort.

"That's what I thought," Rick said raising his eyebrows dramatically. "I just wanted to be sure all was well before I got stuck sitting next to you for five hours."

The two sat quietly for a while, both absorbed in their respective business. Rick was going through the unfinished manuscript making some edits and was happy with what he had so far, but he wasn't sure where to go with it without having a solid investigative thread for his main character to follow.

He looked up from the screen and said blankly, "Do people want to read about an unsolvable crime?"

"That's not the question, old pal," Ian answered as if this was a conversation they had been having. "The question you should ask yourself is this: Does anyone read anymore?"

"Hmmm. Good point," Rick said dryly. "I wish I had a printout of this crap that I'm writing so that I could dramatically throw it into the aisle."

"My point is what do you care about the reader? Do you think they care about you? If someone reads the book or whatever you end up with, it's because they wanted to read it. Maybe they won't even get through it because they hate what you wrote? Maybe they'll even hate you personally for no reason? Well, you can forget about them, and then you can fucking forget about all of the rest, because those people weren't going to read it anyway! Just focus on your real audience."

Ian had a way of making the most preposterous suppositions sound somehow logical. Rick loved that about him and had to admit he needed this pep talk no matter how ridiculous.

Rick's fingers were poised at the keyboard now. "Could you repeat that, please, so that I can record your wisdom for future generations?"

"Very funny, Rick, but you know I'm right," Ian said quickly. "Do you want to write this damn book, or do you want to second guess yourself directly onto the $1 rack at The Strand?"

"I would be lucky to end up on that rack. At least I'd be on a rack, and someone might stop and say, 'Oh, I've never heard of this author. I wonder why?' Then maybe they would buy the book and use it to keep a potted plant from marking the countertop or wield it heroically to swat a hornet."

"I'm guessing this book you're writing isn't a comedy, my brother?"

"More of a 'dramedy' mixed with angst-ridden observations on life," Rick said with mock seriousness.

"Well, I will read it from cover to cover even if it causes me to fall into a deep depression," Ian said cheerfully.

"That's all that I could ever hope," he said patting him on the shoulder. "Thank you, Ian. I do appreciate it."

They sat staring at their screens for a while longer, and Rick broke the silence. "Amanda was asking me, 'Why Iceland?' Of course I couldn't answer her."

Ian looked amused. "I didn't tell you, mate? I've got my fingers in some lava pies. You know about geo-thermal energy, right? Well, that's second only to hydro in Iceland which is more profitable. Less overhead. But what if you could go deeper and hotter, further down into the lava? They're doing it already, and it's possible geo-thermal could overtake hydro in output for less overhead if they can get it right. It's a natural, supercritical steam generator, man!"

Rick had never heard Ian talk about his business dealings with any detail let alone with this much excitement, and his enthusiasm was contagious.

"Great! Deep lava drilling. So much cooler than shoes," Rick said. "I like the sound of this."

"Yeah. Everyone likes the sound of a deep, hot hole, aren't I right?"

Ian always took things down to the lowest possible level when he didn't want to talk about something anymore. It was usually off putting enough that people happily changed the subject. Rick fell asleep, and the flight was touching down at Keflavík as he opened his eyes.

Ian was on his feet quickly when the plane stopped rolling, and by the time Rick reached up into the overhead bin to get his backpack he was already halfway up the jetway. They were now on Ian time which always ran slightly ahead in every zone. He was walking quickly to catch up but got stuck behind a young couple holding hands. He wondered if they were on their honeymoon by the way they were looking at each other and it made him smile despite his fear that Ian had already gone on without him.

He wondered why Ian was rushing, since he still needed to wait for his luggage, and spotted him in the distance standing near the carousel with his arms folded listening intently to something a very large blond man was saying. He gestured toward Rick and said something in the man's ear as he draped his arm across his huge shoulders.

"I thought I lost you there, mate. This is Karl. Karl, this is Rick," Ian said.

Karl smiled at him looking as if he were sent directly from central casting for the role of viking pillager and outstretched his huge hand for him to shake saying, "Welcome to Iceland, Rick," in perfect American newscaster dialect.

Rick said, "thanks," with a slight amount of surprise, and Karl laughed.

"I'm from Reykjavík, but my father was an American airman during and after the war, so I went to school on the base, went into the military myself, and ended up staying here. I just look like Leif Eriksson."

Ian laughed nervously and said, "Karl is my man in Iceland. He's going to drive us to the nearest bar, right Karl?"

"Sure," Karl chuckled. "The night's just getting started if you guys are up for it."

Ian draped his arms around each of their shoulders practically pulling Rick down to his knees and said, "Oh, we're up for it. Isn't that right?"

Rick smiled at the two of them groggily and said, "Sure, why not?"

"Good because I took the liberty of booking us rooms above one of the noisiest bars, so you have zero chance of sleeping before 3 a.m.," Ian laughed.

"Luckily this is just a Tuesday night. The big crowds don't come out until Friday," Karl offered.

"I'll be gone by then," Rick said softly.

"Tonight we begin our adventure, old pal," Ian said quickly to drown out Rick's last comment.

Karl seemed to be driving very fast, and Rick couldn't really see where they were going through the tinted windows in the back seat of the large SUV. He imagined he was actually an unwitting hostage and wondered, "Why does it always feel like I'm being kidnapped when I go somewhere with Ian?"

Before long they'd pulled up in front of a place with no visible name other than a neon sign that said "BAR."

"You guys go ahead, and I'll bring the bags up," Karl said. "I got the keys already."

"Karl is awfully efficient," Rick thought.

"Alright," Ian said loudly, "Let's have a drink, Gordon!"

The place was only about half full as Karl had predicted, and Rick was glad he didn't have to elbow his way to the bar. Ian weaved past some young couples who looked like they might be from out of town and possibly in a tour group. They were clumped loosely in the center of the room as if they wanted to maintain the proper polarity in order to stick together. Ian was waving at the bartender and gesturing for Rick to follow with his other hand like a maître d'.

"Let's have two shots of your finest brennivín, my good man," Ian said cheerfully.

"This looks like it could be toxic," Rick said as the shots were set down.

"Nonsense, old pal, this is the way to the heart of Iceland. It's a shortcut. Puts the fire down below," he said as he downed his shot and slammed the glass on the bar.

Rick followed suit, wincing slightly as the memory of yesterday's shots came flooding back.

"OK. Let's do this," Rick said quietly.

Ian smiled. "So you see now. This is our saga. New vikings in an ancient land."

Karl walked in and moved through the tourist group deftly, without slowing down, and joined them at the bar silently.

"Let's make it three now," Ian said with even more cheer, and Karl waved the bartender off.

"I'm good with a beer," he said smiling. "I meant to tell you, there's a change of plans. We're going to the site by helicopter and staying there overnight. Problem is there are only two seats."

Rick was staring at the bottles along the back of the bar half listening thinking Karl's accent almost sounded midwestern. Then it sunk in what he was actually saying. He would be on his own without Ian.

"Maybe this is good," he thought. "I can walk around the city a little bit and try to get some work done."

Ian wasn't taking the news as lightly. "This is ridiculous," he yelled over the music. "I have my old pal here. I can't abandon him."

"It's fine, really," Rick said. "We'll have dinner Thursday night before I go back. You go do what you need to do. I'll stay here."

Ian had the faraway look in his eyes that usually meant he was hatching a plan.

"I'll be right back. That brennivín goes right through me."

He walked toward the bathrooms and stopped briefly to talk to a woman waiting on line for the ladies room. This didn't go unnoticed by Rick. He always kept his eye on Ian, and the incident at the bar with Merv the other day had just reinforced the need to remain vigilant on this trip. He came back a few minutes later smiling widely and waved the bartender down for another round.

"That must have been some piss," Rick said dryly.

"I'm just happy to be here with you, mate," Ian yelled over the music as he grabbed him by the shoulders shaking him with mock excitement.

"Alright, I get it," he said grabbing his head. "My brain is rattling around in my skull right now."

Ian poked him in the back and said, "Don't look now…" and then dramatically under his breath, "she's at 10 o'clock."

Rick was puzzled. "Your 10 or my 10? Your 10 means there's someone over my right shoulder."

"Yup, that's where she is, over your right shoulder."

Rick turned his head slowly the way people do so that no one will notice they're looking, and there was a very attractive woman standing right there staring back at him smiling.

"Hello! Is everything OK with your neck?"

He was still holding the awkward, craning position and said, "Hi. I was just stretching it a little and there you were. Nice to meet you. I'm Rick."

Ian pulled Karl aside, and then it was just the two of them standing there. She had long and wavy blond hair, and her red cheeks made her face stand out in relief under the dim, yellow light of the bar.

"I'm Lindi," she said as she shook Rick's hand and held it long after a handshake normally comes to an end.

Rick smiled as he gently broke her grasp and said, "Lucky Lindy."

"Well, I don't know Rick, do you think you'll get lucky, or am I supposed to be the lucky one? You are rather presumptuous," she whispered in his ear.

"No. I mean, no! Of course that's not what I mean. They called Charles Lindbergh 'Lucky Lindy.' He was the first pilot to fly solo across the Atlantic Ocean. I often pull out archaic references in conversation, and then the hilarity ensues," Rick said chuckling meekly.

"That's OK, I feel like I might have gotten lucky already," she said warmly as she touched his arm.

Rick was thinking this was more than luck. This had Ian's fingerprints all over it.

"Did you meet my friend, Ian?"

Ian was hunched over the bar talking to Karl who was faced in the other direction. He looked up nonchalantly and said, "Yes! We did meet over by the bathroom. I'm sorry, I didn't catch your name."

"Lindi."

"Ah, 'Lucky Lindy' it is," Ian said without missing a beat.

"I also said that," Rick said flatly as he stared Ian down.

"Sue me," Ian whispered loudly in his ear. "I told her you thought she was cute but were too shy to go over and talk to her. You know what? I didn't lie."

As Ian said "lie" he held up his index finger for emphasis like a professor making a point. Rick gave him one more look of disgust and turned his attention back to Lindi offering her the stool next to him. She sat down with a big exhale of relief as if she'd been on her feet all day.

"My name is really Berglind, but the nickname for that is Begga, so I liked Lindi. It's a struggle. My mother is very traditional Icelandic and doesn't approve."

She was very cute, and Ian was also correct that he would never have approached her on his own. Lindi lived in Reykjavík and worked the day shift at a restaurant on the harbor. She was out with a few friends after work and had the next day free as it turned out. Ian overheard this and jumped into the conversation.

"That's perfect! Why don't you two kids make a day of it? You can take the car, and we'll take a cab to the heliport, right Karl? They can take the car. It's all set," Ian said enthusiastically.

"Sure thing," Karl said with a little less gusto. "Take a road trip. You two have some fun."

"Ooh, I have a good one in mind," Lindi said shifting from foot to foot with excitement. "Can we, please?"

Rick wasn't sure this was a good idea.

"You want to commit to a whole day with me, Lindi? We just met 10 minutes ago," Rick blurted out.

"What better pair to go and spend a day together than two people who've just met? It's fun!"

Lindi's logic was impressive, and Rick couldn't argue. They agreed to meet in front of the bar at 9 a.m.

Chapter 18

The next morning felt like a continuation of the last one for Rick. His hangover had never really gone away. It just became a little different on the third day; more persistent, like a visitor who'd overstayed and begun wearing the host's clothing.

Rick stepped out of the door, and Lindi was right there smiling and waving as she squealed, "Are you ready for a fun ride?"

Rick winced uncontrollably at her high-pitched exuberance.

Lindi reached out and touched his cheek trailing her fingers up to his temple and through his hair. "What's wrong sleepy head?"

Rick smiled broadly as all of the hair stood up on his arms and neck. Looking at her rosy cheeks and red lips in the sunlight, he realized that he was, indeed, ready for a fun ride despite his compound hangover and the jet lag. Lindi was a bundle of energy, and it was hard to deny her. He didn't even know where they were going, but he was ready to follow her anywhere in that moment. She linked arms with him, and they walked toward Karl's enormous SUV.

"Well," Lindi said, "do you mind driving? I'm a better navigator."

"Sure," Rick said confidently, "you just tell me where to go. That's fine with me."

Lindi cheered and ran around to the passenger side as he got behind the wheel and moved the seat and mirrors from Karl's settings. Rick sensed he wasn't too thrilled about his car being used for this "fun road trip" that Ian concocted, so he wanted to be sure to bring it back in perfect condition.

Lindi started directing them out of the city center with a series of rights and lefts forcing Rick to steer through a few narrow back streets. He still hadn't asked where they were going and was silently congratulating himself for letting this impulsive adventure happen. He liked contemplating the unknown but didn't like surprises. Even as a child he was more of a quiet dreamer. He'd dig a small hole in the yard, find a button, and wonder whose shirt cuff it once held closed. He had also found a rusted out clump of a handgun and wondered who'd dropped it or buried it and why. He wanted to become an archaeologist until he realized much later that he had no aptitude for the precision hand-drawn renderings of sherds and shards that the job required.

Lindi requested one last right-left turn combination, and they finally emerged onto "the one" as she put it. This was the main road heading northeast from the city, and they'd follow it for the next two and half hours as it hugged the coast past nine or 10 roundabouts and through two tunnels built under the fjords. The road didn't feel like a "Route 1" to him as they made their way along coastal hilltops and through low valleys. He tried not to stare at the incredible scenery for fear they'd plummet over the side. Vast lava fields with their cone-shaped volcanoes in the distance gave way to vistas of mountain peaks that never seemed to get closer. There were no guard rails or shoulders, only a quick drop-off providing the double thrill of discovery and impending death. Lindi put her hand on Rick's knee, and he flinched a little as he realized he had the steering wheel in a death grip.

"What is your full name, Mr. Rick?"

"It's Gordon," Rick said. "My full name is Richard Gordon."

"Aha! You've lied to me. Richard?"

"Please, call me Rick," he said laughing nervously as he scanned the road ahead for curves and sheep.

"OK, Rick Gordon," Lindi said as she patted his leg. "You look very nervous. Are you alright?"

"Oh, sure. No problem," Rick said giving her a quick sidelong glance. "Just trying to enjoy this beautiful day and keep us alive."

He said the last part under his breath, and Lindi laughed.

"Don't you want to know my name, too, Rick Gordon?"

"Of course, I'm sorry. That was rude of me. What is it? Berglind…"

"It's Berglind Karlsdóttir," Lindi said cheerfully.

"That's a nice name," he said glancing over and smiling at her quickly.

Lindi changed the station on the radio and started patting his knee to the beat of the music. The song sounded like traditional Icelandic folk music until he realized it was a rendition of Simon and Garfunkle's "The Sound of Silence." They drove on listening to the eclectic mix of music and didn't talk much except when Lindi shouted the instruction to keep following "the one" at each roundabout. Finally Rick couldn't take it anymore and asked where they were going.

"I'm proud that I made it this far," he thought.

"Oh, that's silly," Lindi said laughing. "I didn't tell you where we're going?! It's a great place. My ancestors came from this place. My great, great grandfather on my mother's side was a farmer. We're going to Snæfellsnes."

Loosely pronounced, "snayfullsness," but with a slight "t" sound produced by the double "l," the name describes a large peninsula dotted with a few seaside villages and farms. The region is named for a central figure in one of the most recent Icelandic sagas.

"Most people go to the Golden Circle to see all of the sights, the geysers and waterfalls, but you can't do it all in one day comfortably. Snæfellsnes is like a shrunken version of all of it. Here you can see it all," Lindi said happily staring out the windows pointing out the scenery. "Besides this is a real road trip and not some simple tour."

Rick looked at her face glowing, her lips and cheeks somehow even happier and redder as each signpost pointed them forward and further out onto the peninsula. They laughed about the music on the radio, and she reached out and held his hand while they drove.

"Pull in here. Let's get out and walk to the top," Lindi said excitedly.

They were at the base of the Saxholar crater within the national park encompassing the glacier to the east and expanses of lava fields protruding into the north Atlantic on the west. Several lava cones once created the rocky shoreline and the flows and fields of ejecta that surround the base of the glacier. A gradual staircase had been built up the side of Saxholar to protect it from the damage of foot traffic.

"The red lava rock here was once mined and hauled off for road projects, but the government has since decided to protect it," Lindi explained proudly.

The wind picked up as they walked up the cone, and Lindi was holding him around his waist with her hands in his coat pockets. This made it hard for Rick to walk, but he didn't mind her hands all over him. They both tripped on the last step catching themselves on the railing as an older couple was beginning to descend.

"We're exploring," Lindi said excitedly.

The woman looked at Lindi and then at Rick with a slightly lascivious wink and said, "Have fun, you two!"

He hadn't thought about it until now, because everything happened so quickly, but there was a bit of an age gap between them. He figured she was in her very early thirties at the most but looked much younger. As much as Rick didn't want to admit it he was starting to look mid-forties and maybe a little older. Now the two of them were at the top of a volcano alone together, and he wondered once again, "How did I get here?"

"Look at this view! I wanted to tell you a little about the saga from this place," Lindi said. "You want to hear it?"

She looked up at him and smiled sweetly as she thrust her frigid hands under his sweater and ran them over his bare chest. He jumped back and to the side to get away, but she shadowed him refusing to let go.

"Just give in, Rick. My hands are cold!"

"I don't even feel them anymore. I don't feel anything, actually," he said with mock sadness as he hugged her closer to get warm.

She looked up squinting past him into the sun and pushed him away.

"What do you think, I'm some kind of easy Icelandic chick?"

"I didn't know that was a thing here," he said with enthusiasm as he continued to hold her close.

"Just don't be fresh, Mr. Gordon," she said mischievously as she pulled her hands off of his chest and turned to gesture toward the glacier. "Do you know who lives up there?"

"Someone with really cold hands?"

"No, silly boy, well maybe his hands are cold. Always cold, perhaps? He's known as the protector. His name is Bárður Snæfellsás," Lindi said with reverence.

Bárður Snæfellsás, pronounced approximately "Parthoor Snaifullsauce," was the hero of one of the later settlement sagas, and these old stories were more than simple fables to many of the modern Icelandic people. They were true stories from the early times. Lindi was getting more excited as she talked and didn't seem to mind the biting wind that had picked up off of the ocean as she summarized the early part of the saga. Bárður's mother was human, but his father was half risi, or giant, and half troll. He married and had three tall daughters, Helga, Þordís, and Guðrún. Bárður's half brother lived nearby and had two sons, Rauðfeldr and Sölvi.

He was listening carefully trying to remember all of the names and relationships but had to interrupt to ask: "Does half troll and half giant balance out? Is Bárður an average sized guy?"

Lindi laughed and put her finger over his lips.

"Sorry, please go on. This is really interesting," he said.

"Well, as I was saying, the two sons were playing along the shoreline one day around some pack ice. Rauðfeldr pushed Helga out onto a large piece, and she drifted all the way to Greenland. She fell in love there."

Rick was looking intently at her as she talked and was lost in the passion she had for the subject.

"Are you with me, Rick?"

"Yes, I'm listening. 'She fell in love there.' What happens next?"

"Bárður was very angry even though he found out Helga was safe there and had found her true love. He broke his half brother's leg and drove him away to another land and then killed his two sons. He brought Helga back here, but she couldn't bear to be without her lover. After that, he went to live in that glacier that's named after him, and he became a guardian of the people here. They say he wears a grey cloak and carries a long cleft staff to walk the glaciers."

She finished with a slight crescendo like a tour guide at the end of a presentation.

"That's an amazing story. So, I guess no one lived happily after that, right?"

"Not every story has a happy ending, Rick," Lindi said with a seriousness he hadn't seen on her face all day.

"I know. I'm sorry, I wasn't making fun of it. I guess I was just hoping there would be more of an upside at the end. I'm an ugly American," he said apologetically.

Lindi laughed and playfully punched him in the arm.

"No, you're a cute American to me. You're the kind who I don't want to get pushed off the shore on an iceberg so that I never see you again. Know what I mean?"

"You mean I'm Helga?"

"Well, I would say more like Hagard," she whispered in his ear as she gave him a quick peck on the lips and began running down the slope two stairs at a time.

Rick hadn't noticed the elevation and open exposure to the side of the cone going up, and it was a long way down to the bottom. He tried to chase her with his bad knee grinding on every step and prayed that he wouldn't trip and slide face first on the sharp lava rock.

Lindi looked over her shoulder and screamed, "Help! He's gaining on me!"

Rick felt pain through the back of his knee, and it gave out a little. He had to stop, even though he was enjoying her little cat and mouse game.

"Are you OK? I'm sorry if I did that to you," Lindi said with concern as she climbed back up the stairs.

"No, Lindi, I did that to myself, or my self did it to me. I'm not sure, but it's not your fault. I'm not much of a runner anymore. I feel like you've also got some years on me. How old did you say you were?"

"I didn't, Rick."

"Right, that's why I don't know."

"I'm 28," she said with mock despair.

"OK, that makes sense. That's why the woman who saw us at the top gave me the once over and a wink. I'm all out of whack and don't know how bad I look and how good you obviously look in comparison. I graduated high school when you were born, little girl," he said mournfully.

"Well, I've caught up with you, Rick. I'm a woman, and you're a man."

"Thank you for the refresher, but I still feel old next to you Lindi. It's not you. It's my hangup as we used to say back in my day."

Rick stood there for a moment thinking about what it meant to be a man and a woman and how much the definitions and responsibilities had changed over the years. The hunters and gatherers had become homogenized, and no one knew who was who anymore.

"Well, I feel great standing next to you, and you don't look old to me," Lindi said in a singsong voice as she continued down the staircase.

Rick followed at a slower pace wondering what it was he'd done to deserve the affection of this wonderful, visually challenged young woman. She hardly knew him. He still didn't know why Cille wanted to see him. His dating life had been a patchwork of experiences that didn't knit together. He was looking for some kind of cause and effect; some sign that he had done it the right way or at least given it his best shot.

"Maybe right now is it," Rick thought. "What if this girl and her volcano and the glacier troll-giant are all trying to tell me that this is it. They're telling me I should say 'yes' to something good for once before it slips away. Maybe?"

Lindi was running in place in the parking area punching at the air playfully when Rick finally made it down the staircase slightly winded from the effort.

"You're going to need to be less chipper if you're going to keep up with me."

"I can dial it back a bit," she said seriously going into slow motion jogging and punching mode.

"Perfect," he laughed. "Do you feel like lunch?"

"Sure," she said, "I know a good place in Ólafsvík on the northern end. It's on the way out from here anyway."

The road turned north and then east through the peninsula providing a constant view of the glacier, and Rick thought about Bárður in his grey cloak wending his way with his crooked staff across the frozen landscape to help those in need.

"Not a bad legendary existence if you can get it," Rick thought.

The restaurant in Ólafsvík was on the water, and he had the best fish and chips he'd ever eaten. Lindi ordered a big mutton burger with cheese. He was impressed that she planned to eat all of it, but she was finished before him.

The ride out took them over switch-back mountain roads, and Rick was back to white knuckles again. Lindi tried her best to distract him by pointing out the vistas as they made their way through the pass. She took pictures through the driver's side window with him in the foreground to capture all of the views.

"This way you'll be able to go back and see everything that you're missing," she said with a laugh.

"Not to worry," he said, "each blind curve, sudden dip, and sheer drop-off is written in my memory. I'll have wonderful nightmares about this ride for years to come," he said.

"You are too tense," she cooed as she leaned over and rubbed her hand slowly up and down his right thigh.

"You're right," he shuddered as he felt her hand creeping toward his crotch. "My neck is very stiff."

"Oh, I have just the thing for you," she said sliding her hand away, "and it's near this road. I can't believe I didn't think of it before now. Just keep going."

Rick felt like he was a teenager again, except he was old enough to know better and fairly certain that he was just about to do the wrong thing.

"She's right," he thought. "Why can't I just relax?"

He couldn't remember feeling completely at ease around many women in his life. He always felt the need to please them which meant he never allowed himself to relax and just be himself. He didn't really know who "himself" was when he was with a woman, but he knew this was not him. He felt that he owed it to himself, to this version of himself, to try and play the role like an understudy who hadn't learned the lines or blocking because he was sure everything would be fine. The show would surely go on while Rick was happily waiting in the wings hoping for the best.

He glanced over at her, and she was smiling radiantly with her legs crossed on the seat playing soft air drums on her inner thighs to a smooth jazz version of The Bee Gees' "Stayin' Alive." She lazily mouthed the words and became more animated during the chorus. Then she noticed him looking at her and laughed.

"What, you don't like my musical stylings?"

"No, I like it," he said as he averted his eyes from her thighs to the road. "I'm envious of your dexterity and overall musical prowess."

"I think we're getting closer," she said as she snapped back into navigator mode. They'd come to a split in the road: right would take them back out onto the loop around the peninsula; left was the road back to Reykjavík. "We need to go right," she said definitively. "We drove right by it before. Just a little further. Onward!"

He thought about asking her exactly what was a little further, but he was reveling in his newfound impulsive side.

"Here," she said urgently. "Pull off to the left there onto this road."

Rick was dubious. There was an old farm house and a small sign on the fence that said, "Skjálg," but there was nothing else around. The crater Eldborg loomed further in the distance, and its lava field spread toward them like thick, flat fingers.

"Are you sure? There's no sign here, and it's a dirt road. I can't screw up Karl's car."

"Don't worry," she said casually. "This is the road, and he won't care about the car."

"I'll be sure to tell him you said it was OK," Rick said dryly as he continued along the road.

"You can pull in up ahead there. Welcome to Landbrotalaug, Rick!" There wasn't anything within sight, but Lindi took his hand as they got out and said, "Here, follow me."

She led him down another dirt road that became a smaller footpath. There was steam rising from a small, shallow stream which they crossed using some short planks that had been laid there. As with many places in Iceland, the earth itself seemed to be alive. There was a lot going on just beneath the surface. The strong sulfur smell hanging in the air was a constant reminder that the ground below their feet was ready to become something new. A small stone protrusion was about 20 yards ahead with more stones piled around it, and she let go of his hand to sneak up and peek around the other side.

"We're all alone! Let's get in before someone comes," she said excitedly.

Rick had allowed his new, impulsive side to catch his old boring self by surprise.

"Get in? Get in what?"

"That's what you do in a hot pot, silly. It's a hot spring built for two, see?"

Lindi was already pulling off her jacket and pointed down at a small, circular opening in the rocks.

"Oh, I didn't bring a bathing suit," he said as he realized what was coming next.

"Neither did I, silly," she said as she pulled her sweater over her head.

"Oh, umm, right," he stuttered as he started to take his coat off slowly and tried to think of a reason to stop removing his clothes.

"Hurry up, Rick," she said. "You won't regret it. It's going to feel great."

Lindi had never stopped taking off her clothes while Rick was stalling and was now down to nothing but her woolen socks. He tried to look away, but she was even more beautiful than he'd imagined. She was dancing from foot to foot in the cold wind smiling and laughing at him as she pulled off each sock and added them to the pile. She turned around, thrust her perfectly round, white-pink cheeks in Rick's direction, and lowered herself gracefully into the steaming spring.

"Oh, come on," he thought. "This is it. The understudy is on!"

He took off all of his clothes without talking or stopping and stepped quickly around to the side of Lindi keenly aware that he was naked outside in front of a beautiful young woman but trying to convince himself that it was all completely normal as long as he pretended it was no big deal.

"Finally," she said with exasperation as he slid down carefully next to her.

Lindi put her arm around his shoulder and gave him a quick peck on the cheek. The water was clear and ran continuously to top off the pool as it overflowed into the small stream that led away from it. He could see her body crouched down, her skin looking like wavy pearl as she moved her legs next to his. They were up to their shoulders, and Lindi turned to face him and took his hands as she wrapped her legs around him.

"I want you to kiss me, Rick," she whispered looking at him with her eyes half closed as she slid toward him.

Rick wanted to argue. He wanted to be back in New York with Pippa, walking the streets, lost in his thoughts; lost in other people's thoughts and dreams and things of other times. He wanted to see Cille and hold her hand. He wanted a lot of things, but he knew he needed to kiss Lindi right now. This wasn't something he could simply not do, so he leaned forward and didn't think about it anymore. He thought only about the moment and not what happened in the past or what might happen next. They kissed, and Lindi put her arms around his neck and pulled him toward her tightly. Then he felt her hand trailing up his leg until it was wrapped around him.

"Well, I see there's been some kind of volcanic chain reaction here," Lindi gushed as she tugged her hand and moved her lips to his neck making small bites toward his earlobe.

"Um, I'm not sure we should go any further," he said nervously. It was a mix of anxiety and something else, but he couldn't figure out what else was bothering him besides the fact that he really cared for Cille. He was taught he wasn't supposed to care like that after one date.

"Aww, don't be that way, Rick," she said in a pouty voice. She took his face in her hands, looked at him seriously, and said, "Is it my father?"

"No, it's not…wait what do you mean is it your father?"

"I thought maybe you're weirded out by it," she said.

"Why would I feel funny about your father? I mean it's certainly a consideration," he blurted out. "Now that I think of it. Any father would say, 'Nobody's good enough for you.' I think I wouldn't want you to date me, actually. Does your father know you go on day-long excursions to hot pots with older men who have no bathing suits? You don't have to say…"

"Well, you've brought him up already on this trip, so I just assumed he was on your mind."

"When did I mention your father? I think I'm missing something here," he said rubbing his head.

"You were just worried about his car, you silly. I told you he wouldn't care," she said as she kissed him roughly a few more times on the neck.

Rick's eyes shot wide open as he realized what she was saying, and he put his head down as far as it would go into the water.

"She's Karl's daughter," he thought. "She said her last name was Karlsdóttir. That was a big hint, idiot. That's how they traditionally name children."

"You don't feel frisky now," she said flatly and moved as far away as possible from him in the small space.

"I'm sorry," Rick said slowly, "I didn't know. I guess I'm the only one who didn't know. I'm just catching up here. I'm sorry. That reaction has nothing to do with you, Lindi."

"Well," she said sadly, "I guess I can understand the confusion. I can see how you would also feel strange because of it."

"Yes," he said nodding hopefully as she spoke, "I'm just feeling a little strange right now, and it's certainly not because of you."

"You are a funny, silly man, Rick Gordon. Give me a few more kisses before we put our clothes on again."

Rick thought about making a break for it at this point, but he figured he'd never have a chance to kiss a beautiful woman in this particular hot spring again. He also didn't want to completely shun Lindi after the revelation that Karl was her father.

"It actually wasn't a big deal," Rick thought trying to convince himself.

He kissed her again holding her head in his hands, stroking her wet blond curls and pushing them behind her ears. He rubbed her shoulders and kissed her neck. He didn't know what he was trying to do because he wanted it to be over, but he felt too attracted to her to let her get out of the pool. He didn't want this moment to end. He was being selfish now which was also a new trait.

Lindi moaned lightly, and suddenly there was giggling and shushing coming from behind the rocks. Rick stopped kissing her, and then three heads popped up. A mother and two teenage daughters had come to enjoy the water. Rick was not exactly ready to exit the hot spring in front of them, but Lindi got out shamelessly like a true Icelander, and he figured that was the best distraction he'd get, so he got out right behind her.

The girls giggled while Rick struggled to put on his pants. He had his back to them, and he hoped they'd also turned away, but then he realized he didn't care whether they saw his ass or his balls. If they were looking, they deserved to see them. Why should he care? He considered this another breakthrough into this new, impetuous part of his personality that he'd never known before.

After they'd dressed, said awkward goodbyes, and extended well-wishes for a pleasant soak to the mother and daughters, the two walked back to the car without talking. Rick was trying to figure out whether to punch Ian or just give him a strongly worded rebuke. He wondered whether he already owed Karl an apology simply for what he had been thinking about doing with his daughter. He hadn't thought about it, but it was perfectly logical for Karl to have a daughter her age.

"I could practically have a daughter her age," he thought.

He realized his disgust was misplaced. Karl's daughter was an adult. She knew what she was doing and didn't need a chaperone. She liked Rick, and Rick liked her. She liked Rick a little too much and too fast for his liking, but he was very attracted to her which made it even harder to accept. He thought he had more self control.

"OK, that was fun," she said in a chipper tone. "Back to Reykjavík for us, right?"

Lindi seemed sad, and Rick felt like an idiot. They drove back along the coastline and didn't talk for a while until they got to the first tunnel. The sudden change to artificial light seemed to shift the tone, and Rick spoke first.

"Lindi, I think you're incredible, and I don't know what the hell you see in me, but I know you're something special. I've had a lot of fun today."

"I've had fun too, Rick," she said. "I still don't want you to go floating across the sea on your iceberg."

"We'll always have Snæfellsnes," he said as he took her hand. "Thank you for a great day."

"Great memories," she said with a small smile as she closed her eyes and fell asleep.

They got back quickly, or at least it seemed quick to Rick. Once she woke up, Lindi was quieter and kept her air drumming and lip syncing restricted to Queen's "We are the Champions" when it came on the radio a few miles outside of the city.

Rick parked the car where he had found it, and Lindi told him he better hold onto the keys since she was working a double shift the following day.

"I may not see you before I leave," he said softly as he reached out to touch her arm. "I'm looking for a flight back as early as tomorrow afternoon if possible."

"Oh, so soon? Your iceberg is melting perhaps and you're afraid you won't make it back in time?"

Rick looked at her and closed his eyes as if to divine the future. "No, I'll make it back to New York in time and I'll be back to Iceland again someday. It's a two-way iceberg."

He held her hands and leaned down to kiss her cheek.

"I'd like to believe in you and your magic transatlantic iceberg," she said, "but I know when I see a melty one. You need to get home before you get stranded somewhere in between."

She said this matter of factly, without a hint of sadness, and, once again, it was hard to argue with her logic. They said goodbye on the sidewalk outside the bar where they'd met, and she kissed him on the cheek.

"Look me up if you do make it back here," Lindi said over her shoulder as she turned to walk away.

Chapter 19

Rick sat on the edge of the bed taking deep breaths stretching his arms over his head and behind his back.

"Still tense," he said to himself. "I wonder why?"

He laid back on the bed and laughed uproariously for a moment before starting to softly cry.

"Hmmm, I'm a mess," he thought. "Lots of emotions going on here, but why? I'm so pissed at Ian. I'm mad at myself. I let down all of mankind by leaving Lindi in the hot pot like that. I miss Cille and Pippa. I miss the Green Door. I want to go back to the bar and tell Ian and Merv and the frat boys in the corner that I'm not going on this trip, but what would that solve? I am the problem in all of this, and I can't blame any-one but myself."

He got up and went to the bathroom to take some aspirin and caught his visage in the mirror. He didn't even look his age anymore. He stared into his own eyes looking at the wrinkles around and underneath them and grumbled, "What was Lindi thinking, anyway?"

He tried to rationalize all of it and decided he was up against cultural differences and his own shyness. He laughed to himself thinking about Lindi's attitude about nudity. He'd never used a beautiful naked woman as a human shield before.

"I'm just a prude, and she's the normal one. Case closed," he said to himself.

He looked up the next flights to JFK and found one at 10:30 the next morning. He sent a note to Ian apologizing for his quick departure and thanking him for bringing him along even if it all didn't work out as planned. He left the last part hanging there for Ian as a clue to his irritation at being set up with Karl's daughter without his knowledge. He knew Ian would never understand why this angered him, so it wasn't worthwhile to make a big deal of it. Rick had tried to pry apologies out of him over the years, tried to prove his point to him, but Ian always demurred when apologizing was all that was left to do. Part of his magic was his ability to remain blameless; maintaining plausible deniability at every turn by convincing others to become culpable themselves. He was like Professor Harold Hill from "The Music Man" with his uncanny ability to effortlessly sway everyone around him to his way of thinking.

Now that Rick had some time to mull it over, he knew approximately what Ian would say: "Rick, you never would have gone with her if I told you she was Karl's daughter. You looked scared of him when you met, and quite rightly. He's a killing machine, you know that right? He spent his career killing people. You owe me if you think about it. She's beautiful, am I right? How did it go, anyway…"

Rick laughed at the one-sided mock debate he had conceived. He knew Ian so well that he could have continued for a while. No, it wasn't worth anyone's time to hold a grudge about it. He decided the new Rick Gordon was going to spend more time enjoying the present. He just needed to get back and find a way to finish up the storyline before it drove him crazy.

The Ridley dreams came every night, and they were always just about the same, putting him tantalizingly close to the second murders. It had become a game he would play in his dream mind to get down the stairs faster, but something always kept his legs moving slowly; as if the air itself had split into thick waves of time pushing back like a wind, relentlessly driving yet undetectable. He would reach out to grab the wall along the staircase to propel himself faster, and sometimes stumble down a few steps feeling as if he were falling in slow motion, but he never made it to the opening of the doorway in time to see the cause of the sickening thud and the gunshots followed by the woman screaming. It was always, "What was that?" in a high-pitched voice, and Rick was grasping to parse what it all meant.

It wasn't getting him any further with the writing, so he wanted to know why he was having the dream more than he needed to know what it meant. It felt as if he was forced to relive the same moment over and over for an important reason, but then he would wake up and not understand why any of it mattered. He was always back to the beginning again, and he didn't see a logical end in sight unless he just offered his own idea. There were numerous theories that were perfectly plausible, and he went over them one more time in his head.

It could have been Ridley himself who just got angry enough two times in his life to kill his private secretaries when he realized he was being swindled. It could have been Weinstein all along who coveted Moench's job for its easy access to embezzled funds and kickbacks he'd probably been receiving during Prohibition from the bootleggers using the secret room. Did Weinstein end up on the receiving end of his partners' greedy intentions? It could have been the woman scorned, or the woman in love with another man, or maybe Weinstein had another wife who found out he was leading a double life with his Mrs. Lee in a the hotel on 38th St.? It could have been a coincidence that the gun ballistics looked similar given the rudimentary tests in the early 30s. Many guns in those days were chambered for a .32 caliber round including a popular police service revolver manufactured by Colt. Perhaps the "same gun" theory was hatched by one of the 36 detectives on the case in order to expedite the closing of it, since they realized there was a lack of physical evidence and no more leads to follow?

Rick's theory, the one he was having his character follow, was a hybrid approach. It relied more heavily on the early bootlegger connection because he felt that was the one slight split in the road the police hadn't taken. Clearly, there was fraud being committed overtly by Weinstein and his partners with their shadow companies and the attempted fake will. It could very well have been the two of them, with or without an accomplice, trying to cut out Weinstein's piece of the pie in a desperate money grab when they realized they'd have to wait for Ridley to die of natural causes. They also may have realized that surviving family would likely dispute the will and prevail once it came to light that there was $200,000 earmarked for Weinstein who had only been in Ridley's employ for two years. That didn't match old Ridley's modus operandi, and to prove otherwise would be tough. It would require hard evidence that Goodman and Hoffman didn't have. They would need something akin to Ridley being visited by three ghosts resulting in a Scrooge-like shift to beneficence.

He stopped for a moment and thought about all of the other places someone could have planned to kill Ridley given the fact that the old man was such a creature of habit. Then he figured that the cellar office was probably the best spot. Ridley had become a regular sight on the way to and from the office, and almost invisible because of it, but people were always around him during his daily commute, whether they paid close attention or not, right up until he descended the stairs each morning into his cave three levels below the street. Ridley's private grotto undoubtedly felt safest to him, but it ended up being a his own prison for the next 30 years before eventually becoming his grave.

Rick needed to send his main character down a path that made sense but also didn't feel too obvious. He surmised that there could have been more organized crime activities besides bootlegging going on around the garage. Ridley wouldn't have known what was happening once he left each day to catch the 3:30 p.m. train back to Fanwood. Moench and Weinstein's brother who ran the garage would have had free reign to do what they liked with the space until Ridley arrived again around 9:30 a.m. the following morning. If this were the case Moench may have gotten too close or too greedy. Once Prohibition ended there would have been a vacuum created by the loss of the bootlegging business that could have quickly been filled by gambling and loan sharking. Clearly, Moench and the Weinstein brothers could have been involved enough to at least turn a blind eye to the bootlegging. A mob connection also explains why 36 separate detectives failed to close any of the cases.

"Dead men tell no tales, and cops who want to live don't make certain arrests," Rick said to himself as he shook his head. "Is this any good, though? Another mob story. Nobody cares anymore."

He kept turning the possible murder scenes over in his head imagining them as if the different players entered and exited comically through side doors with the lights maddeningly fading to black every time there were gunshots. The persistent dreams were disturbing enough in the nightly, repetitive loop they presented, but his waking imaginings of the events had also become frustrating because they were only creating more confusion.

He'd started to think of his main character as a sort of imaginary friend, and he was afraid of letting him down.

"I'm sorry," he said softly toward the keyboard, "I'll get this together for you. You can count on me."

Rick had decided to name his protagonist Ian since he represented a much more exciting and intrepid version of himself. He had thought about changing it after what just happened with Lindi, but there was no point in that. His Ian was not exactly a real-life Ian. He was more like Rick with a different personality. He knew everyone who read it and knew him or Ian would see similarities, but much of that would be in their own imaginations.

"Everyone wants to be a character in a book," he thought, "and everyone thinks the author must have had them in mind, but it's usually just a combination of people or a version of them that could never exist in real life. People are types no matter how individual they may feel, and we all want to recognize a little of ourselves in others."

He started typing faster now that he'd decided to go with the organized crime plot. He planned to have Ian go back to the murder scene and poke around. In the story the garage attendant, named Wong, was more amenable to Ian's request for access to the basement, and he'd allowed him to go down and explore after some suave small talk. Wong also really liked Ian's little dog, Max, which helped seal the deal. Things went a lot smoother for Rick's main character than they did for him in real life. He'd thought about re-creating the scene, but no one would have believed how rude Hyung had been, and they certainly would never believe he just happened to meet the love of his life while standing outside as his dog urinated on the wall. No, his Ian would go down into the basement that day. Even if there were a Cille-like character trotting by on the sidewalk for him to meet, he would have already been down the three flights feeling along the dank wall as he looked for signs of the old office. Ian was there to sniff out treachery and death not love.

"Ian certainly wouldn't have fallen in love right away like a fool even if a naked girl ran right into him on the staircase," he thought.

He'd been lost in thought for a while and suddenly felt as if as if he'd forgotten to do something important. After fishing his phone out of his bag he noticed he'd missed a text from Cille.

Hi, Rick! I'm coming home early. So tired of this job and this place. Still can't breath :(All is well though. Maybe we can meet Friday if you're home early enough!?

He smiled for the first time in hours and replied to tell her he couldn't wait to see her and was also coming back early. It was only 8:30, but he started to fall asleep almost immediately as he laid back on the bed and put up his feet.

Chapter 20

Rick had intended to take advantage of the uninterrupted hours on the plane to move the story along a little, but he ended up sleeping the entire trip. There was a brief smell of lunch being served that nearly roused him, but he was exhausted from the night before and didn't budge as the cart went past.

He hadn't realized how many decibels the music and rowdy patrons generated in the bar downstairs while he was in the midst of it. There were a few hours of peace until the crowd started to gather. Laying there, trying to force himself to sleep, it sounded like he was inside the bar, as if his bed was just sitting in the spot where the tour group had clustered together the night before. He'd been in the country for 36 hours, and he'd slept for about four of them. He thought about Lindi and her melting iceberg theory and figured it was just her cute challenge to come back someday to prove her wrong. He knew he had been too quick to leave such a beautiful place, but he was happy to be going home to see Cille. He also missed Pippa more than he thought he would and was slightly worried about how things had been with Amanda. He had to remind himself that she wasn't "party all of the time" Amanda anymore.

Once they landed he let her know he'd be on his way to pick up Pippa. She texted him back while he was dropping off his bag at the townhouse.

Oh, I thought you told me I could have him until Saturday?!

Rick looked at his phone shaking his head.

I'm coming for him in about an hour, OK?

There was a brief break, and then he saw that she was typing again.

But we had plans later.

Rick laughed.

You and Pippa made plans? What are you doing? Can I join you?

It was mani pedis. You wouldn't like it. See you soon!

Amanda was barefoot and wearing her standard pajamas when Rick arrived around 3 p.m., and he gave her the obligatory once over.

"Is this your late afternoon to evening collection?"

"You're just envious of my chilled out lifestyle," she said defiantly.

Pippa was curled up in Amanda's bedroom at the opposite end of the apartment when he heard Rick's voice. He came spinning around the corner sliding across the marble floors before gaining traction on a throw rug and then spinning out on the marble floor again before finally reaching him and rolling over on his back.

"OK, little guy, I missed you too," he said as he patted his belly while a stream of urine shot into the air like a small fountain.

"Wow, he must really like you," Amanda said with surprise.

"Yes, he knows who he can really trust in this world," he said dramatically. "He trusts I won't get mad when he pees on me."

Pippa rolled around ecstatically and then started barking until Rick picked him up. They'd never been away from each other since he'd gotten him as a parting gift from Claire. The two of them had been together constantly since then. They had become life partners in a small way because they only had each other. Rick cradled him like a baby and whispered in his ear.

"Did you have fun with your Aunt Amanda, Pip?"

"Yes, I did, I really did," Amanda said in a cartoonish ventriloquist voice.

"You taught him to speak so quickly! Thank you!"

"So, you're back early? What's the deal. You and Ian get in a fight?"

"Not particularly. It was fine. I just wanted to get back home," he said nonchalantly.

"You couldn't wait to get back and curl up on the couch with Pippa? What's your deal, Gordo?"

"Sure, of course, other things, you know," he said shyly and then quickly covered with, "I just went along with Ian because he wanted to spend another day or so together before he left for Singapore. Didn't really work out."

"What 'other things' are you planning? I'm just curious."

"Nothing special," he said casually. "Oh, I do have a second date this weekend with a nice girl."

He had hardly gotten the word "date" out when she raised her finger to interrupt.

"Oh, um, excuse me, I had a feeling there was a woman in play here. I know you, Gordon. I know the faces you make when you're falling for someone. The way you talk about them. What's her name?"

"It's Cille."

He knew what she meant by the face. He could feel it happening now.

"That's the face," she said as she turned and walked into the kitchen.

"OK," he conceded, "so perhaps I'm doing it again, and maybe I'm not? She's really great, and I wasn't even going to tell you about her for a while. That's how much I care about her."

He realized how bad it sounded just after he finished saying it.

"Oh, sure," Amanda said dryly, "as if telling me about her could jinx it, and I suppose I have somehow had a hand in your previous relationship debacles and bad breakups?"

"You're right," he admitted. "I don't think it's you. It's me, and I didn't want to hear you telling me that it would once again be my fault in the end. I was just delaying the inevitable. I do hope this time it works, though."

"Let's toast to that," Amanda said handing him a bottle of water. "You really deserve it, Rick."

He packed up Pippa's things and put him into his bag for the subway ride home.

"Thanks again," he said as he carefully hugged Amanda around the neck.

"You're not going to crush the baby or anything. I'm not that 'gordo' yet, Gordo," Amanda laughed as she grabbed him in a bear hug and said, "Hey, how's the book coming along?"

"I'm getting close," he replied confidently even though he wasn't sure how it was going to end.

"Well, I want to read it first," she said as he was walking into the elevator. "Did you base a character on me?"

"Several of them," he chuckled as the doors closed.

Rick sighed as the two reached the sidewalk, and he turned toward Central Park instead of the subway.

"Maybe just a little walk to clear our heads, Pip?"

Pippa let out a series of staccato barks, and Rick set down the bag to let him run on the grass once they were in a safe spot. He ran in circles until he started to orbit Rick too widely and it looked like he might intersect with runners and bicycles. He ran over to grab him, and Pippa ran back to meet him halfway jumping into his arms at full speed and landing with a little squeak. Claire had mentioned she had him do some agility training at the fancy daycare where he was enrolled as a puppy. That was before they had met, but Rick saw it come out every once in a while like an old trick that the new dog had just remembered.

"Are you ready to meet Charlie tomorrow, Pip?"

Pippa looked at Rick quizzically as he heard this questioning tone of voice and snuck a lick of his cheek. He nuzzled his face into Rick's shoulder, cooing softly, and they walked to the subway.

They pushed through the turnstile, and a lone woman on the platform said, "Look at that precious little dog."

Rick looked at her and smiled, but she never made eye contact with him. She kept her gaze on Pippa for a few more moments and walked away.

"Good thing I'm not relying on you to be my wingman," he whispered to Pippa as they boarded the F train. "Although I'm pretty sure you were the reason Cille stopped running that morning, so good job, little buddy."

Pippa snuck a quick lick of Rick's cheek again, nuzzled himself back into his shoulder, and let out a small sigh just as he had after they first met Cille outside the garage on Allen St.

"Let's go home and take it easy, Pip."

They approached 12th St., and he took him out of the bag to walk the last block. The gingko tree next to the stoop had unfurled seemingly overnight giving the facade a very calming look as the leaves cast small spots of shade that danced along the windows. Rick couldn't wait to take a nap but was awake as soon as he got inside and back upstairs to the secret room. He knew he couldn't fall asleep right away, and he poured himself a few fingers of rum to hasten the process. He turned on the monitors, and all of his research popped up slowly on the screen as the windows reopened. He didn't need it anymore, but it was a quick look at where he'd started. He looked at the old articles he'd pulled up and realized he'd done everything he could to get to the center of the mystery short of going back in time to witness it himself. He zoomed out a little on one of the articles and looked at some of the surrounding news items wondering what other mysteries lurked there. He checked the bookcase behind the couch for something uplifting and opened *Wuthering Heights* which was Emily Brontë's only novel. The label inside showed the symbol "Cf," and the back of the card said "Catfish-Sativa."

"Call me Heathcliff," he said as he inhaled deeply from one of the smallest of Ian's glass bowls. He was particularly amazed at Ian's inventive marijuana pairings given the fact he'd never read any of the books on the shelf.

The words continued to come fast now that he was focusing on the possibilities that came with the organized crime connection, and he worked for several hours until he thought he knew what would happen next. He didn't know how much he'd written, but he knew it was the most he'd gotten done in one sitting. He picked up Pippa, who was curled up by his feet, and they went to sleep just before 9 p.m. as Cille was landing at Newark airport.

Chapter 21

Rick didn't bother setting an alarm because Pippa had always been a reliable wake-up service. He was startled awake by the usual dream and then saw light streaming through the curtains out of the corner of his eye. He wasn't sure where he was waking up at first, and then he saw Pippa's tail next to his head and realized he was back in New York. It was much later than the usual breakfast time, and he attributed this lapse in normalcy to Pippa's two-night stay with Amanda. She wouldn't have put up with his early rising. She always woke up late, and it was often too late to get where she needed to be. She'd made a sport out of it over the years, sometimes winning and other times suffering devastating losses.

She was fired from her first job for her chronic tardiness, but everyone in her life at the time sloughed it off as Amanda being Amanda. She was just out of Skidmore and had gotten hired as a PR coordinator for a small book imprint. She thought it was the next logical move after her undergraduate degree in English literature with a minor in public relations. Despite her chipper attitude and witty repartee, the publishing house fired her after six months because her attendance was setting a bad example for other employees even though she was getting all of her work done. That was when she settled on law school. Once she'd researched the different job types within the legal profession, and taken her own personality into account, she decided to look for a job as a corporate attorney. She believed this would keep her as insulated as possible from long hours and big-firm politics, and most of all it would limit prolonged, close-up exposure to people. Rick figured there was a protracted "wake up" period for Amanda now that she didn't even need to shower, and she was only limited by her supply of clean sleepwear.

"OK, little fella," he said as he moved Pippa gently from between his legs where he had curled up after migrating from the pillow.

He looked at Rick with a yawn that ended in a high "oohhh" sound.

"It's going to be a more exciting day than that, Pip," Rick yawned as he picked him up and flipped him onto his back to rub his belly. "We're going to meet Charlie today and see Cille again."

Pippa looked at him and barked his little half squeak, half air combination he'd begun to use when he didn't feel like giving the full effort. He noticed Pippa had started doing it the day they'd met Cille, but he wasn't yet sure what this new vocalization meant.

Rick's phone rang loudly in his hand, and it startled him. It was Cille, and he felt the same small twinge of excitement in his stomach that he had when he'd called her the first time. They agreed to meet by the fountain in Washington Square, and Rick sprang out of bed leaving Pippa behind wrapped up in the blankets.

"We need to get ready now, Pip," he said over his shoulder as he hurried down to the kitchen to make coffee.

There was a warm breeze carrying a slightly floral aroma as they opened the door to leave, and the sun seemed to shine like a spotlight on the stoop. It was an idyllic spring morning, and Rick closed his eyes and took a deep breath feeling the sun on his face and a deep sense of calm until Pippa jumped against the railing and barked angrily at the sparrows chirping in the gingko tree.

He said, "OK, you won that battle, Pip," and they turned and walked to Fifth Ave.

He spotted Cille sitting on the far edge of the fountain as soon as they walked past the arch. She was looking intently in the other direction, and he could tell Charlie was straining at the leash barking at something just out of sight. As they got closer, the subject of Charlie's scorn came into view. There was an old-fashioned organ grinder with his monkey standing on a small folding table next to him. Pippa caught sight of this before Cille saw them coming, and suddenly there were two miniature dachshunds side-by-side ready to attack a man with an exaggerated, fake mustache and his small, defenseless monkey.

Cille was laughing and had just gotten up to drag Charlie away when she turned to see Rick next to her trying to reel in Pippa.

"Well, they have a mutual distaste for monkeys in tiny hats," she said laughing. "They're off to a pretty good start."

Rick stood looking into her eyes for a few moments too long. He was lost in them and realized too late that he needed to greet her in some way. He put his arm around her shoulders and kissed her cheek at an angle, stood back from her with a look of shock on his face, and said, "Well, that's not how I imagined this."

"Hmmm," she said as she grabbed the back of his neck, got on her toes, and pulled him close to her as they kissed.

There was barking and loud laughter in the background, but Rick and Cille didn't care. Neither of them had felt this excited by anyone since they were teenagers, and they had both assumed this was something only teenagers experienced until they felt it again here in the middle of Washington Square Park in front of everyone. Rick realized the laughter was directed at them when he looked up to see Charlie chasing Pippa around attempting to hump him while they had been brazenly making out.

"I'm sure they just thought we were doing some kind of performance art," he whispered in her ear.

Cille looked at him with a gleam in her eye and poked him in the ribs.

"OK, little Miss Charlie," she said in a loud, theatrical voice, "you leave nice little Pippa alone, and stop being so forward on the first date."

There was a burst of loud laughter at this from another group of tourists standing between them and the organ grinder.

"Let's take a walk," he said reaching for her hand.

He had the bag just in case, but Pippa and Charlie seemed perfectly happy walking along in tandem sniffing everything the other one sniffed along the way. The first dog date was going well for everyone involved except for the humping incident.

Cille squeezed his hand a few times and smiled as she looked at him.

"So, how was your trip?"

He thought about telling her the entire story including Lindi but figured it could wait. Rick postulated that it wouldn't be a big deal that an attractive young woman had her hands all over him, and around him, in a thermal pool once they knew each other a little better.

"It was quick. Interesting," he said. "My friend Ian is not the best companion. He sort of left me, so I went for a ride the one day I was there with his business partner Karl's daughter, we ended up in a hot spring, and…"

Cille interrupted with a laugh, "Wait, is this the beginning of your submission to Penthouse Forum?"

"No, I promise that's just about where it stops sounding anything like porn."

They both laughed and she said, "I don't care what you did in the hot spring. I wouldn't blame you if I'm imagining Karl's daughter the way you were about to describe her."

"How do you know so much about these things, anyway?"

"I have an older brother, silly boy," she said pinching his butt. "He didn't know I found what he stashed under his mattress. You can't shock me."

"I always forget there are people who have siblings or cousins around to teach them the ways of the world," he said. "I didn't have that in my life, although my second cousin Jackie visited one summer and covertly handed me her tattered paperback of *Forever* by Judi Bloom. I was probably 12 or 13, and I do remember keeping it in a shoebox under the bed. The spine was already worn at all of the good parts, and I could open up to each good place if I gently fanned the pages."

Cille laughed, "I had that book hidden under my bed, too!"

"We were so innocent in comparison to the kids today."

"Yes, but we had to try harder. Today it's too ubiquitous. I mean we had to try to find anything sexy, so it used to mean something when you held it in your hand."

He stood next to her watching the dogs sniff at the base of a tree and realized he was still holding her hand. They were nearly at Houston St., and he'd held her hand the whole time. He started to feel uncomfortable and pretended he was looking for something in his pocket.

"I'm sorry, I'm not really a hand holder. I mean, I don't normally hold a hand. Your hand was nice, you know what I mean," he stammered.

She laughed and said, "I suppose we can never go back to holding hands now!?"

He realized how crazy that must have seemed and took her hand again for the next few blocks before finding a convenient time to let go when Pippa stopped short and Charlie kept on running.

"So," he said trying to catch up with them, "tell me how was your trip?"

Cille turned to look back and rolled her eyes.

"It was interesting, that's for sure. One of the models pooped in a hot air balloon."

She walked on calmly and let that image hang in the air like a cartoon with aroma lines emanating from it.

"I see why you came home early," he laughed.

"Well, let's just say that was the poop that broke Cille's back."

"It was a mighty poo," he said in the style of a documentary voiceover.

"You want to know? Here's what happened," she said. "These girls are almost always a problem, let's just say that, but there's one I've worked with on a few other shoots who is always extra trouble. Mya is very nice, but she's always getting into something. One time there was a rat in her room in Belize. Well, it was a rat according to her, scurrying behind the walls, and she trashed the room. I mean she really trashed it like she was Keith Moon or something. I guess she had golf clubs with her, and she just kept banging away at the drywall with her sand wedge until she was covered with gypsum dust and so was everything else. That was fun. So, anyway, we had a sunrise balloon shoot on the schedule for Wednesday so that we could do it again on Thursday if we didn't get it right. On Tuesday night, Mya went out with one of the crew and ate Thai food. She posted from the restaurant and captioned a picture of her Pad Thai and Green Curry, 'Ballooning tomorrow morning. #hopefullynopoop' and then proceeded to tell everyone else on the shoot when she got back from dinner that she was concerned she was going to have to go to the bathroom on the balloon. That lasted until we were getting ready to drop the ballast (no pun intended), and the gondola was lifting off the ground. Then she seemed to be at ease. She seemed oddly resigned to the fact that she couldn't go to the bathroom for the next hour or so. Then she started saying it."

"What did she say?"

Cille paused, and Rick looked at her waiting for the rest.

"She had to take…" he said trying to help it along.

"No. It would have been OK if she said that," she said shaking her head.

"Well, what did she say?"

Cille gritted her teeth. "She said, 'I need to go poopies.' She kept whining over and over again. There were eight of us in the gondola including the pilot. All of us probably need therapy now."

He thought about that for a moment and started to chuckle.

"It's an odd phrase, most definitely, especially for an adult who is announcing something to other adults that's already extremely embarrassing. It's compound embarrassment."

"She started to get a little frantic and ran around the gondola in a circle shaking the rails as she went. We thought we were going down. Then she asked if anyone had a tissue, and I was thinking, 'Since when is one tissue enough for something like that?' Right? Then, before anyone could stop her, she picked up one of the sand bags the pilot had inside the gondola for ballast, cut it open with a small knife she produced from her purse, and emptied half of the sand over the side. She then proceeded to squat down over the half-empty sand bag, and…I'm just saying this girl had no shame. She did it right there."

"She went poopies," he said in his most gravely serious documentary voice, "all with the help of her trusty pocket knife."

"That's gross, stop. Please don't say it again," she begged.

"Done," he said gently as he patted her on the shoulder, "now would this be a bad time to take your mind off of that with a kiss?"

As he said it his mouth was already on hers, and he didn't care who was looking. He knew he must be falling for her if he had this kind of reaction to the story she just told. He grabbed the back of her neck, and she pushed herself against him. By the time they looked down, Charlie was trying to hump Pippa again, except this time he was letting her do it.

"My dog is very comfortable with his sexuality."

"I'm sure he's quite virile," she said with a smile.

"Was that the end of the story?"

"Pretty much," she sighed. "You had to be there, but that's when I decided I was going to quit."

Rick tried to keep it up with his documentary voice and said, "By the time the ill-fated hot air balloon descended to earth, she knew it was time to call it quits."

"You can stop that, now," she said flatly.

"Wait, you're actually resigning over this?"

"Not exactly. There were other things, other signs that I should quit. I don't enjoy it at all anymore. That was a big sign."

"Well, I trust you're making the right decision. At least it's on your own terms."

"I've been thinking about it for a while. I have a few old clients who've asked me about doing consulting work. I've saved a lot, so I'm not concerned."

"I need to figure out my next move," he said seriously. "Too early to retire, and I can't crash at Ian's place forever. Although, I suppose I could sell the house in NJ and become a hobo who wanders train tracks with his bindle over his shoulder."

"What about your book?"

"Well, I can't expect to earn any money on it," he said quietly.

"Who cares? Finish it, put it out there, and take it from there."

Her voice rose to a crescendo, and both dogs barked and jumped on her leg.

"They think you're mad at me."

"Just don't worry about money," she said quietly.

They walked on until they reached Canal St., and then turned back to head north on Sixth Ave. It felt like they'd just started out from the fountain where they met, but they'd already been walking for nearly 30 minutes. Pippa had been holding up well, but he stopped in his tracks and looked at Rick, wagging his tail, as they waited to cross Houston. He happily scrambled into the bag when Rick lowered it, and Charlie tried to climb in with him, but there wasn't enough room. She kept getting pushed back out by Pippa when she'd try to wriggle inside.

"I think we're gonna need a bigger bag," she said, and they both laughed and hugged each other not noticing that the light had already changed.

Rick stood on the traffic island holding her tightly, sensing the pedestrians brush by them, and wondered when he would stop feeling like a teenager. Charlie jumped against the back of his thigh barking and Pippa poked his head out trying to nuzzle himself between their faces.

Rick had always been keenly aware of his surroundings, wanting to know who was nearby, wondering what they were saying or thinking in the moment. He had been picked for the safety patrol in elementary school because of this tendency to look out for others, but they didn't realize that it was more than empathy. He was really looking out for himself as he tried to fit in and poked around for openings. Being on the safety patrol with his orange belt and silver badge didn't win him any friends, and it was the last time he ever volunteered to look out for other people. After that he just observed others and their interesting behavior as a hobby. But right now, standing there as the light changed again, he didn't care about anyone besides Cille. Everyone else faded into the background and became insignificant. He decided this was an even better personal achievement than the newfound impulsiveness he'd detected on the car trip with Lindi.

"I think I may have finally caught that fish that my friend John was talking about," he thought. "I just need to reel her in slowly."

Cille looked at him and smiled and took his hand to cross Houston once the light had changed again.

"I know this sounds crazy," she said reluctantly, "but I feel like I'm starting to fall in love with you."

Rick felt a tear in his eye. He'd wanted to say the same thing. Instead he made a joke because that somehow seemed safer.

"Well, that is the normal second-date reaction that I get."

Cille laughed, and he put his hands on her cheeks pulling her close to whisper in her ear.

"I didn't want to say it myself because I didn't think it could be real. I don't know what it is, but I'm just going with it. I love you, and I'm afraid of what will happen if I start to feel it any more than I do right now."

He kissed her, and they looked at each other, and then they kept kissing. They stood embracing on the corner of Minetta St., and Rick imagined he could feel the current of the old stream as it flowed below their feet and continued across to Downing St. and the Hudson River beyond. He never wanted the moment to end, and he didn't care if the water appeared once again and swept them away. Pippa started to whine, so Rick put him down with Charlie who sniffed him and licked him this time instead of trying to hump him.

"This is progress," he said pointing at Charlie who had begun grooming Pippa's face and ears with her tongue.

"I think they like each other," she said in a dreamy voice.

"Hmmm, I think so," he said taking her hand, "let's go and give them a break from all of this walking. They can get to know each other better. Actually, my knee is killing me right now. We can stop at Ian's place. My place. OK?"

"Sure, but I only fall in love on the second date. Nothing else happens. I can only have one big thing happen per date."

"I wouldn't have it any other way," Rick said gallantly as he kissed her hand.

Chapter 22

Rick and Cille woke up beside each other the next morning, and every morning from then on, with Pippa and Charlie wedged in between them. Sometimes they stayed at Cille's place in Stuytown, but they usually slept at the townhouse because it was more fun for the dogs to have the run of four floors. The two of them had also enjoyed having the run of the place, and Rick was hoping Ian wouldn't show up again unannounced.

Summer had passed them by, or they allowed summer to pass, as they continued to bask in each other's company. They didn't leave the city once, and suddenly it had gotten close to Thanksgiving, which meant it was time to meet Cille's family, and Rick wasn't feeling very sure of himself. Even though he knew they'd accept him, there was always a part of him that felt like an orphan. Cille's family was big and close, and he'd never had a Thanksgiving that required a kids' table. He was hoping to blend into the crowd. There would be about 15 adults and six children there there according to Cille.

They packed up her car with both dogs and two apple pies and hit the road for the small town of Andes, NY that was infamous for the anti-renter movement of 1839. Rick was keenly interested as Cille explained that rent had been allowed to go unpaid by the local landowner until he died and his will authorized his heirs to collect decades of back payments from the area's farmers. It was a feudal system in every way. Farmers had a limited amount of good soil to work with to grow the wheat they owed the landlord. Rioters, or revolutionaries as they preferred to be called, often disguised themselves in homemade "Indian" costumes harkening back to the Tea Party of their grandfathers' day.

"People don't really come here to commemorate or re-enact the events as you might imagine," she said with a laugh as they turned onto a two-lane county road.

He saw an old-fashioned "fountain service" sign as they came around a bend and said, "Let's pull in here for a minute."

The sign and the front of the luncheonette looked almost identical to the one where Rick had spent many afternoons as a teenager. He stood for a moment shielding his eyes to block the glare as he looked through the window expecting to see old Frankie standing behind the counter smoking a cigarette. As he got closer he could see the interior had been converted into a convenience store with a small deli counter, an overhead cigarette display, and lottery machine. Cille stood by the door waiting for him to follow her inside.

"I don't even want anything, so I'm waiting for you, mister."

He was still standing at the window peering inside.

"I thought I'd go to the bathroom. Maybe get a soda. Want anything?"

"Sure, I'll get something," she said as she opened the door. "You're acting a little funny."

He realized he was acting funny and downplayed it with his absolute worst Joe Pesci impersonation.

"So, I'm funny how? Funny like a clown?"

"More like you're hallucinating or something, sweetie," she said nervously.

They walked through the door, and there was a strong, almost acrid, odor of mold. That smell always hit Rick in the face like a punch, but he was well aware that it didn't bother some people. For him it was more than just a smell, it was a sign that someone had given up and let the mold win. He remembered his mother was also very sensitive to it when she took him to the garage sales around town.

"Ricky," she would say under her breath, as she handed him an old book or a framed print, "this smells musty, right?"

He smiled as he remembered those simple, summer days with his mother, just the two of them with the classified section of the newspaper and the addresses circled in blue pen. Some of the sales would have exclamation points on the right and left side of the column, and those were always the first stops. Every house had a smell, but the smell of mold was the only one that really bothered his mother.

Cille was tapping him on the shoulder asking, "What are you thinking about, sweetie? What do you want to get?"

"Hmmm, I was just thinking I'll skip it," he whispered. "It's musty in here."

"Oh, yeah, I guess it is," she said.

They each got a bottle of iced tea, and the teenaged clerk rang them up without glancing away from her phone. After a few minutes back on the road, Cille closed her eyes and fell asleep. The old fountain service sign had brought Rick back to the late 80s. His parents had been gone for about five years, and he already had his first girlfriend and first breakup before the summer between eighth and ninth grade. He started smoking cigarettes regularly when he was 15 despite the fact that he'd always hated the smell. In some ways, it felt like a connection to his parents, and it was a habit he would continue for the next 25 years. He only thought to quit when Uncle Will was diagnosed with cancer, and his own mortality came into sight as he prepared to lose his last real connection to his parents.

The luncheonette was a regular weekday stop for Rick that summer. He always went by himself, parking his 10-speed outside the window, and he was usually the only patron besides a few of Frankie Ward's cronies sidled up to the counter. They never seemed to order anything, but Frankie was always ready with a smile and a full pot of coffee. The friends sat huddled together, and their low, conspiratorial tones followed by uproarious laughter sounded like the ebb and flow of the ocean to him. It was the sound of old friends, and he wondered if he'd have people like them to drink coffee and laugh with when he got to be Frankie's age.

Rick figured he was in his 70s. His father had operated the luncheonette before him, and there was a photo of the two of them on the wall behind the counter with Frankie standing on the sidewalk out front in his Navy uniform, his arm draped over his father's shoulder. The windows behind them were filled with ads for war bonds, and Frankie was smiling with his dark, wavy hair flowing out from under his blue cap. It wasn't clear whether the photo was taken at the beginning or end of the war, but Frankie and his father were smiling widely, so he always assumed it was a homecoming and not a farewell.

Rick's father had also served in the Navy during World War II, and each time he went to the luncheonette he thought he might try to strike up a conversation with Frankie. Walter Gordon had never shared much with his son about that time, but Rick had an album filled with photos and memorabilia from ports across the south Pacific, and Uncle Will had shared the small amount of detail that he knew. The most memorable story involved Taiwanese beer tainted with formaldehyde, which Uncle Will said was the reason his brother always drank vodka. Each time they were alone in the luncheonette, when Rick thought he had the nerve to call across to Frankie behind the counter and ask him about his service, one of his friends would walk in and sit down at the counter. Rick wasn't confident enough to talk to Frankie with another old timer there. He was afraid they would laugh at him, but it was all in Rick's head. It would have made their day if he had asked about the war, but he never thought about it that way at the time.

Frankie was a tall man and had remained slender after all of those years. He seemed to tower behind the counter and hunched over it to compensate. There was a high, marble countertop with leather-topped stools and a soda fountain, a few tables, and a wooden phone booth in the back corner. Frankie would always have big beefsteak tomatoes on top of his white Philco refrigerator which he also seemed to tower over, and he proudly showed them off to Rick every time he came for lunch that summer. He would usually order egg salad on whole wheat with a slice of the tomato, and Frankie would look benevolently at him, like a friendly neighbor at a picnic, as he handed him the sandwich across the counter.

Rick could tell by the look in his eyes that he had seen a lot. He didn't realize it then, but Frankie's wife had passed away a few years before. He never thought about whether he was married or not. He'd never even been introduced to him as Frankie, but that's what all of his friends called him when they walked into the place. Rick could picture him now, leaning over the counter, his filterless Lucky Strike cantilevered off the edge of his two fingers, a thin but warm smile on his face as he sipped his coffee. There was something in his eyes that Rick should have recognized. He was lonely then, wrapped up in trying to become someone, trying to make it through being a teen, wanting it all to speed up to the next chapter or whenever the happy part started. He thought only about himself, and maybe he cared a little about what Frankie and his friends thought of him, but he wasn't aware enough to realize Frankie might have been even lonelier.

"He was a nice guy," he said out loud as he brushed away a tear and quickly glanced over at Cille.

She was still sleeping, and he was glad he didn't need to explain why he was crying because he wasn't sure himself. Her family's house wasn't far, but he had to wake her up to navigate once they turned onto the dirt road.

"It's just another 1/4 mile or so, and then you turn right. You'll see a red barn," she said groggily as she quickly checked her makeup in the mirror. "I'm sorry to put you through this crazy Golding family gathering. I know it's a lot."

He smiled wryly and said, "I'm looking forward to it."

It was true that he was looking forward to meeting Cille's close family. It was the logical next step in their relationship, and meeting them all at once was like tearing the metaphorical Band-Aid off of his general discomfort with family gatherings. After his parents were gone, Thanksgiving was he and Uncle Will sitting across from each other at the kitchen table, and, because of that, the two of them didn't usually make a big fuss over it. They both agreed that it seemed like just another day unless you had family or friends with you to enjoy it. Rick also felt the same way about Valentine's Day as he started getting older, but that was easier to spend alone than Thanksgiving. Still, he'd made a turkey every year since Uncle Will had died. It was just he and Pippa, so the leftovers stretched a long way. He'd made one Thanksgiving meal for Claire, but she was gluten free and scrutinized every bite which ruined the whole experience for him. She didn't have a close family, and she wasn't a "Thanksgiving kind of person" she had said as she put her napkin down over her half-eaten plate.

Even though he was nervous to meet her family, he figured the Goldings were a ticket to his first proper Thanksgiving in many years.

"This is it," Cille said studying his face as they pulled into the rutted dirt drive and passed a large red barn.

He could see her looking at him as he carefully steered through the narrow lane and asked, "What is it?"

"Nothing," she said beaming at him. "I'm just so happy you're here with me. I promise no one is going to go all 'Deliverance' on you or any-thing."

He stared straight ahead and grabbed her hand to emphasize the fact that he was also happy to be there.

"Yes, I was hoping we could avoid a situation like that. No whitewater rafting while we're here," he said.

The road split with one branch climbing higher, and Cille directed him to turn right and go downhill. As the road bottomed out, a large house came into view at the end of the dusty lane. It didn't seem to fit the rest of the surroundings they'd passed in the last five or 10 miles. They were in a small hollow now, and there was another large barn off to the side of a pasture that was more modern with fans and ventilation hoods at the top.

He gestured toward it as they parked and asked, "What are they doing here?"

"I think goat cheese, mostly," she said as she got out of the car.

"I love cheese," he said enthusiastically as he detected a slight smell of marijuana on the air.

The dogs had been so quiet for the last part of the trip Rick had almost forgotten they were in the car, but now they were barking and jumping against the window as they saw her uncle's big golden retriever standing behind the screen door. He normally worried about what would happen to Pippa in a standoff with a bigger dog, but he decided to open the back door and let them go running to see what would happen.

After a quick period of sniffing and wrestling, everyone was happy and curled up on the couch. It was a large sectional, and Pippa, Charlie, Rusty the golden retriever, Charlotte the teacup Yorkie, Wally the West Highland terrier, and Otto the puggle managed to monopolize it so that everyone else had crammed into the kitchen and dining room. Her parents came over right away, and Rick was relieved that they seemed to like him. Her father shook his hand and loudly announced he was glad Cille had brought home a nice guy for once and Rick was welcome to her if he wanted her. They all laughed, but Cille didn't find it very funny.

He was fairly at ease with this initial family interaction until he saw a tall man standing in the corner coming toward him smiling and pointing at him using his two fingers to pantomime the "I'm watching you" gesture.

"Who the hell is this guy," he thought, "and where did Cille go?"

Cille was in the kitchen talking with her Aunt Luanne who just had a double knee replacement and was walking around holding the cane like a baton without letting it touch the ground.

"Hello," Rick said as the man approached him with his hand out.

"Hello young man," he said as he shook Rick's hand vigorously, "I'm Lucille's favorite uncle. You can call me Floyd."

"It's really great to meet you, Floyd. So, no Uncle Floyd for you?"

"Sure, you can call me whatever you want, son" Floyd said apparently missing the reference to the beloved New Jersey television personality.

"Alright, let's say you're Floyd and I'm Rick if that works for you?"

"Sounds good, son," he said as he patted him on the shoulder and walked away.

Cille walked over shortly afterward and rolled her eyes.

"Did he tell you he's my favorite uncle?"

"Yes, he did mention that."

"Let's just say I have others on the list above him," she whispered in his ear.

"OK," Rick whispered back, "now here comes someone else. Please don't leave me alone again."

"Oh, look it's Aunt Martha! Rick, this is my Aunt Martha," she said pushing him gently toward her.

"Hello, Rick," Aunt Martha said meekly.

"Hello, it's nice to meet you."

"You caught me at a good time before I'm dead," she replied flatly.

"No, Aunt Martha," Cille laughed, "you're not dying!"

"Not yet, dear," she said with a grin. "I'm just getting you people used to the idea. I'm tired of everyone asking how I am. Love you."

She turned to walk away, and Cille looked at Rick and searched his face trying to divine how he was handling it knowing that there were several more equally odd relatives circulating in their direction.

"I'm OK," he said in her ear knowing what she was thinking. "Bring it on, I say."

"I owe you for this," she said as she moved past him to say hello to two people, and Rick imagined her as a game show host introducing the next contestants.

"Hello," he said stretching out his hand to get ahead of the introduction and save her some trouble.

"They can't hear you! Uncle John and Aunt Marguerite have severe hearing loss," Cille said loudly punctuating each word as she leaned in toward Rick's ear.

"Thanks," he said holding his hand over his ear, "I can hear you, it's them not me."

Rick reached his hand out to greet them, they all smiled at each other, and the conversation didn't go any further because someone made the announcement that it was time to sit down for the meal. There seemed to be a lot more people in the house than he thought once everyone started gathering around the table.

"Maybe she downplayed it so that I wouldn't get anxious," he thought.

"OK," Cille said grabbing his hand, "let's get a seat and some food before both of them are gone."

By the time they got to the dining room, there were only two seats left at the kids' table. Rick pulled out the folding chair for Cille with a flourish, carefully fitting his legs under the card table that marked the border between the adults and teenagers and nine younger children.

The youngest looking blond girl sitting across from Rick started the introductions.

"What's your name? I'm Tiffany."

"I'm Rick. It's nice to meet you Tiffany."

The boy next to her said, "I'm Max," and then screamed "Max" seven or eight times while making stabbing gestures at the ceiling with his fork.

"Great," Rick said nervously as he looked to the brooding, dark-haired girl sitting next to him. "Who else do we have here?"

"I'm Lindsey," she said with a quick smile before frowning again, reeling back, and punching him in the arm.

Another boy on the far side was silent, and Rick looked over at him.

"What's your name?

"I'm Peter," he said in a slightly unsure voice.

"Well, it's nice to meet you, Peter."

The boy's face lit up, and he got up and gave Rick a hug around the neck. Cille was watching him and smiling from across the table, and they locked eyes for a moment amid the loud cacophony of voices at the gathering. He felt the happiness in the room, he could see it on Cille's face, and he realized he'd never experienced anything like this growing up. His parents and Uncle Will loved him and had undoubtedly done their best with family holidays, but it was never like this. There were certainly never this many people in the room.

When dessert was over, and people started spreading out around the house, Cille's cousin Matthew tapped him on the shoulder and suggested they take a walk. It was warm for late November with only a slight fall chill in the air, and the breeze carried a mixture of goats and hay along with the unmistakable odor of marijuana.

Matthew patted him on the back and handed him a large joint.

"Here," he said passing him a lighter, "you deserve this after the kids' table."

"Thanks," Rick said with slight surprise, "don't mind if I do."

He inhaled deeply and handed it to Matthew as they walked toward the barn.

"I wanted to show you what we have going on in here besides cheese," Matthew said as he opened the double doors.

There was an overwhelming odor as soon as the doors opened, and Rick smiled as he looked around at the plants.

"We have a small operation here. Cille said you were cool, so I figured you'd be interested in this."

"Very interesting," he said taking a deep breath. "It smells great in here."

"You're soaking in it," Matthew laughed as he exhaled and coughed slightly. "We started doing this at cost for a collective of people who needed it medicinally, but now it's gotten easier in New York, so we're going to scale back and focus more on the cheese again. You can always come to me for either," he said with a wink. "But, seriously, we're all really happy for you and Cille. She seems like she's glowing. We haven't seen her look this happy in years, man."

"I'm happier than I've been in many years, too, and it's not because you just showed me your barn full of weed. She's the best thing in my life. She's the best thing that's ever been in my life."

As they walked back toward the house someone opened the screen door and all five dogs bounded onto the porch and down the steps.

"We were thinking we might as well get a third one," Rick said watching them chase each other in circles. "We figured it couldn't be much more trouble. This looks like trouble, though."

As he said that, a wrestling match ensued with Pippa and Charlie taking the brunt of the attack from the bigger three while the teacup Yorkie crab walked around the scrum yipping like an ineffectual referee. Pippa and Charlie came out barking from under the Westie, puggle, and golden retriever, and Rick reached into the fray to pull them to safety. He reached down and scooped them up just as Cille walked out onto the porch followed by every child at the table.

She waved and dramatically mouthed, "Let's go!"

She had already circulated around the house and said their goodbyes, so Rick had a smaller contingent of close family bidding them farewell on the front porch. Matthew followed them down the steps as they were headed to the car and handed him a paper bag which he quickly put into the trunk of the car.

He looked at Cille with concern and said, "Would you mind driving?"

"Yes, Rick," she said rolling her eyes. "I can see that you and Matthew had a nice little chat."

"Fun day," Rick said chuckling.

"Thank you, honey. I know that was a pretty extreme family adventure."

"I should thank you! I loved meeting everyone, even that girl who punched me."

They drove for a little while in silence, passing the fountain soda sign again, and following the winding road back to the thruway. The sun gleamed through the windshield onto Cille's face, and Rick had never seen anyone more beautiful.

Chapter 23

Rick finished the first draft two weeks before Christmas at nearly 2 a.m. Pippa wasn't in his old position at his feet but in bed curled up in the crook of Cille's arm next to Charlie. He was relieved to be done with the initial manuscript and wanted to do some editing before giving it to anyone. Cille had been promised the first look, and he was about two days of work away from handing it over to her. The dreams hadn't stopped when he got to the end. They had actually become more realistic, and now it was harder to shake the memory.

There was a growing feeling of urgency each time he made his way down the dream staircase toward Ridley's cellar. The audio of the murder still played the same way each time with the visuals tantalizingly out of sight. Sometimes Pippa was with him to bark, and other times he just stood there on the last step frozen as he heard the gunshots and the thud before the woman's voice. He always woke up as soon as he heard her exclaim, "What was that?!"

Her scream sounded more urgent now. That was the only thing he could think that had changed in five months of maddening nocturnal repetition. He would sometimes feel himself step back during the dream, and imagine that the people he could hear in the office just out of sight were actors recreating the scene for him each night. It was as if the whole scene had to be played over and over for his benefit, and the unseen players were starting to get tired of it.

He had fallen asleep in the secret room with his draft on his lap and red pen stuck between his fingers when Cille came in and made him come to bed. She hadn't let him spend the whole night sitting up in that chair since they'd been together. Both dogs were under the sheets curled up between Cille's bent knees, and he laid next her listening to her breathe rhythmically and softly, exhaling with a soft puff of air and snoring slightly as she inhaled. He smiled and drifted off to sleep.

The dream started differently that night.

Rick and Cille returned to the garage on Allen St. together with Pippa and Charlie. The plan was to have Cille create a distraction while Rick snuck through the door and down to the cellar. Frankie from the luncheonette was the parking attendant, and he leaned over the small desk inside the booth with his leg up on a chair balancing his Lucky Strike between his fingers. He smiled and stared directly at Rick, held up a large beefsteak tomato, and winked.

Cille looked at Rick and said, "I love tomatoes," then walked toward the booth with the dogs, holding them up in front of her to block Frankie's view.

He took that opportunity to slip through the door, closing it softly behind him. The staircase looked different than usual, but he figured that was because he was closing in on the actual scene of the crime.

"Of course this is different," he thought.

Pippa barked from somewhere above, and Rick thought someone was probably coming, so he took a few more steps down looking back and forth quickly between the faint light he could see at the bottom of the staircase and the darkness at the top where he heard barking. He held onto the wall as he went because he couldn't see anything. The faint light at the bottom was gone, and it was dark at the top when he looked up again. He took another step and heard the familiar squeak of the stair tread in the townhouse. Then he heard the woman say, "What was that!?"

He jumped a little and his foot slipped on the tread and it squeaked again as he tried to turn and get away. He was pivoting as he'd always done in the dream trying to follow the usual order: run, wake up, be safe again.

"Wake up, just wake up already," he thought.

Instead he felt himself lose contact with the stairs, and then he was falling, almost floating, through the air until he was laying at the bottom of the staircase feeling tired and still dreaming instead of waking up as usual, and he looked up toward a dim light that let him see into another room.

Now Pippa was barking again from far away, but Rick didn't pay attention because he looked up to see Ridley laying on the floor about five feet away. He peered into the room, but it didn't look as if anyone could see him. There were two men in fedora hats and heavy, black overcoats standing over another man in shirtsleeves who was laying on the floor under an office chair. The woman had dark hair pulled back tightly under a pill-box hat. She held an iron bar in her gloved hand, and it was the same one that he had seen described, along with the stool, as the weapon used to bludgeon Ridley. He laid motionless watching and listening and stifled a gasp when he saw a small rivulet of blood flow from under Ridley's long white sideburns and snake its way toward him.

There was a loud sound like a scream from above along with the sound of Pippa barking. Rick started to slide himself back toward the stairs so that he couldn't be seen by the murderers, but he couldn't move. His legs felt heavy, and he heard more screaming along with sirens.

"This isn't good," he thought. "The cops are coming. Why would I be on the floor here? What's my excuse? What if they see me now? Did I go back in time? Am I really here and seeing this? Who is that woman and the two men?"

His head was spinning, and he felt like going back to sleep so that he could wake up again and leave this terrible dream behind. Then he recognized the faces of the two men under their hats. They weren't mobsters. It was George Goodman and Arthur Hoffman, Weinstein's accountant partners in crime from The Bronx. He wasn't sure who the woman could be unless it was "Mrs. Lee" double crossing him.

"Maybe they couldn't wait for old Ridley to go," he thought, "and they also wanted Weinstein's piece of the pie? Maybe Weinstein threatened to cut them out or wanted to take a higher percentage because of his more important, more legally exposed, role in the scheme?"

There were two more men now, and they were putting Rick on a stretcher. He wondered why no one said anything. Goodman, Hoffman, and the woman in the hat just stood there, and he figured they couldn't see him. It became very quiet, and he felt as if he was having a dream within a dream.

He stood barefoot on the corner of 36th and Seventh as people rushed by in both directions. Most were moving toward Penn Station. It was a summer evening, and there were heat waves coming off of the asphalt, but he couldn't feel his feet. A man with a briefcase and straw hat pushed into him, and he saw his father's face clearly as he passed him with cigarette smoke trailing in his wake. He pulled at his legs to get them to move off of the pavement, as if they were stuck in deep mud, and tried to catch up to his father. The people crowding the sidewalk created a rip current that pulled him further away the faster he tried to run. There was a flash, and he was inside Penn Station running down a set of stairs to Track 1, but Walter Gordon was still ahead of him and too far out of reach.

He frantically yelled, "Dad!" over and over again as he watched his father board the train, the doors closing behind him as he stepped through. He tried to run and bang on the door but couldn't feel his feet again and just sat down on the staircase watching the train pull away.

He heard people talking around him and then felt wide awake, except when he opened his eyes he couldn't see. Things came into focus, and he was standing on a tee box over a golf ball. He was nine years old, and his father stood next to him with his hand on his shoulder. He had hit two balls in a row into the water hazard on a par 3, and the group behind them was approaching.

"Now, here's the thing, Ricky. This is what most people don't understand about golf," his father said calmly. "You stand up and swing that club. Don't tense up, question it, or try to finesse it. Swing the club, and hit the ball. Do it the way you think it should be done."

Rick squinted into the sun, looked across the pond at the flag, and squared off over the ball looking up at his father one more time for reassurance. Walter Gordon nodded slowly and tipped his cap. He took a deep breath, held it, and swung the club. The ball hit the center of the green, bounced twice, and stopped next to the hole, and his father yelled, "Way to go, Ricky my boy!"

Rick tried to follow him, but he couldn't move again. All that he could do was watch as his father continued down the cart path that curved around the pond, fanning himself with his hat as he walked toward the green. Rick heard muffled voices. He sat down, put his hands over his eyes, and cried in frustration. Then everything was quiet.

Suddenly he felt cold water rushing by and he was sitting cross legged in the middle of tall reeds along a riverbank. Light snow was falling, and as he stood up he realized he was just downstream from the old house on Rockaway Creek that Amanda's cousin Rob owned. He was still barefoot and the cold burned into his soles. It was hard to move again, and he sat down in the rushing stream with his legs crossed, holding his head in his hands shivering. He knew he needed to move before he froze and yelled, "Wake up!" as loud as he could, but it sounded muffled as if he were underwater.

He saw a large man coming around the bend in the creek wearing a brown hooded cloak. He was moving silently toward Rick carrying a large staff to steady himself as he stepped effortlessly over the frozen rocks. Rick couldn't move at all now, so he continued to sit helplessly in the frigid stream and watched the man glide toward him. The tall figure stretched out his hand and effortlessly picked him up and out of the water. His legs were warm now, and he could feel the cold water rushing over his feet and ankles again.

He opened his eyes wide and tried to see under the large brown hood. "Are you Bárður Snæfellsás? Have you come to save me?"

The man pulled back his hood slightly and smiled. It was John, and now he was holding a fishing rod and net instead of the long, crooked staff. His brown cloak was suddenly a simple rain poncho.

"I've been wondering when I'd see you back here, son."

"I'm happy to see you," Rick said. "Do you have any idea why I'm here? I can't seem to wake up from this dream. It's a dream, right?"

"I'm not sure," John said quietly as he put his hand on Rick's shoulder. "Want to fish a little? I've got a rod here for you."

John guided Rick downstream with his hand on his shoulder.

"You remember I told you about this spot, son?"

"Yes, I caught one right after you left and released it. Biggest trout I ever hooked."

"Good, that was the right thing to do. Try again now," John said.

Rick held the lure between his fingers trailing his free hand over the barbless hooks under the yellow and black feathered tip. He opened the bail and cast sidearm into the swirl just beyond the big log, closed the bail, and felt a hard strike. There was a flash at the surface, and it was a large rainbow almost as big as the brown he'd caught the last time. John expertly pulled the fish gently into the net and held it just under the water in the shallow channel where they were standing.

"What do you say, Rick," John said slowly as he slid the hook out of the fish's mouth. "Is this the one?"

He looked at John quizzically and said, "Well, at some point we need to choose one, right? Bring home something for dinner?"

"You can't choose," John shot back quickly. "Fish choose you. And this fish doesn't choose you."

"Well, he kind of fooled me the way he jumped onto my hook."

"You need to go home. Time for you to go back home, Rick. Today's not a good day for fishing. It's not your time yet," and then he pointed upstream toward the path that led back to the house.

"I don't want to leave here."

"You don't have any choice," John said softly.

Rick turned to argue with him, but he was already gone. He looked up through the trees and saw a blue heron fly overhead flapping its wings so slowly it seemed to float effortlessly. The snow stopped falling, and the sun was breaking through the clouds. He saw smoke coming from John's chimney as he slogged through the stream, and his feet didn't feel numb anymore as he walked up the muddy bank and found the path back to the house. He could hear muffled voices again out of earshot, and he looked around in every direction to see if anyone was there.

"What was that?!"

He heard it again as if he was still in the usual dream.

"What was that?!"

It sounded more frantic, and he heard other voices mumbling again.

Rick felt a hand squeezing his, and he heard it again: "What was that?!"

There was a blurry shadow of a person leaning over him, and he heard another voice much clearer saying, "Let us look," and bright lights flashed into his eyes.

He felt someone touching his eyelids and saw Cille's face as a blur before another flash of light. Her eyes were red and puffy, and she started to laugh and then cry. Two men in blue shirts standing behind her looked at Rick cautiously. He could hear a rhythmic beep, and there was a strong antiseptic smell. Another blurry woman walked into the room, looked at him very seriously and walked out again curtly telling Cille she would have to leave until the next morning. He fell asleep again to the sound of muttering voices. He was happy that Cille had been there even though he didn't know what happened or why she had to leave him.

He still didn't know where he was or why he was there when he awoke to the sound of shuffling in the dimly lit room. A nurse had come in to check his pulse, and he grabbed for her hand thinking it was Cille's. She pulled away, and Rick opened his eyes just as she was hurrying out of the room. He closed his eyes again and fell asleep.

There was a light knock, and he woke up to see Cille standing in the doorway with the sun streaming on her face.

"Hi," he said with an unexpectedly weak voice.

"Hi, honey," she said rushing over to grab his hand. "I've been talking with the doctor, and he thinks you'll be OK."

"What? OK. Why am I going to be OK? I mean why is he saying I should be OK. Am I not OK? Can you please explain? I was OK yesterday."

"Honey, you fell," she said patting his hand. "Do you remember anything?"

"I remember having the dream and going down the stairs. There was a squeak like the stairs at the townhouse. I saw who killed Ridley, I think."

"OK. Just relax. I can't believe you were sleep walking. It's like a cartoon."

Rick started talking but his mouth was moving faster than his brain.

"Do you think maybe, maybe, you never know, do you think there was a scent trail coming up from the kitchen? Like someone was making bacon and I floated out of bed following it until I fell onto the griddle and hurt myself? That's probably it."

"Probably something like that, sweetie," she said patting his arm.

Rick smiled pathetically. "I always figured that's how it was going to happen, and now look at me," he said pointing at his head bandage.

"You're going to be OK now, Rick. You are in good hands."

"I know, I know" he said quietly and then closed his eyes.

There was a nurse standing in the corner of the room listening.

"He's bound to be confused and groggy for the first day or so after an injury like that," she said gently as she closed the curtain dividing the two beds and walked out of the room.

Cille picked up Rick's right hand and held it to her chest. Glancing around to make sure no one was looking, she leaned over, kissed his forehead, and carefully laid next to him in the bed with her head on his shoulder. She quietly whispered, "I love you," over and over and fell asleep.

Rick was out of ICU that afternoon and released from the hospital the following day. The doctors and nurses said they'd rarely seen such a quick recovery, but they didn't believe he had a typical traumatic brain injury. The neurologist said it was probably more like a deep dream state than unconsciousness. The symptoms were more in line with a mild concussion, and one of the nurses theorized he had avoided a more serious injury because he was completely asleep when he fell. She'd read a study about car accidents that showed injuries were typically less severe for sleeping passengers than those who were awake during impact.

Whatever it was that saved him, everyone agreed that Rick was lucky to be leaving the hospital in such good shape.

"I've been meaning to ask you," he said as Cille pushed him in the wheelchair past the small gift shop and toward the exit, "how did you get into the hospital room?"

"I told them you're my fiancé, of course!"

"I forgot we were engaged," he said rubbing his head. "This head injury stuff is really something."

"No, silly, I lied."

"I'm not sure I can be engaged to a liar," he said in a sad tone. "How did they buy that story?"

"I was crying hysterically. Very convincing. They bought it, OK?"

"OK, I'm sorry I put you through this," he said apologetically. "I mean, why would anyone as sweet and beautiful as you ever agree to marry a guy like me?"

"That sounds more like it," she said with a laugh. "Keep that up, it's working. I might even forget that you're now officially damaged goods."

She pushed him through the sliding doors onto the bright, sunlit sidewalk outside Bellevue just as an ambulance siren squealed by the emergency room entrance. Rick held Cille's hand and they each gazed silently out the window of the cab as it moved through slow traffic on Second Avenue.

"Do you want to stop at your apartment or go home for a bit? You're probably sick of me by now," he said.

She looked at him smiling and said, "No, I won't be leaving you alone for too long at this point. I want to keep you in bed if you know what I mean."

"That sounds nice," he said as the driver looked in the rear view mirror and smiled.

Pippa and Charlie somehow always knew when they were home and were barking and scratching at the door even before they'd made it to the stoop. The two of them clamored to be the first to jump into his arms as the door pushed open, jiggling and barking, wailing, and clawing at his legs to get to him. He sat down on the floor and let the dogs climb onto his chest.

"I missed you guys, too," he giggled as they each licked his face and neck.

"They did miss you," she said. "Pippa kept curling up in the spot where you fell, and Charlie was crying and looking for you in your upstairs room last night."

He picked up both dogs and hugged them to his chest, and Cille left to get some groceries once he convinced her that it was safe to leave him alone. The dogs didn't let him out of their sight and followed him upstairs, shadowing him as he climbed each step, keeping pace rather than running ahead or getting underfoot as usual. He paused for a moment on the squeaky stair tread and stepped up and down on it a few times listening to the sound. The last time he heard it he was on the precipice, hovering between dream and reality, death and life.

Rick sat down on the couch in the secret room, and the dogs jumped onto his lap nuzzling their faces into his belly. He tried to piece everything together from the moment he lost contact with the squeaky stair tread. He didn't have complete recall of everything he'd experienced while floating through his dream state. He knew everything he saw was just a projection of his own imagination and the shadows in his mind. He knew this, but he couldn't shake the image of the three murderers standing over the bodies of Ridley and Weinstein. He moved the dogs onto the chair gently, stood up slowly, sat down in front of the monitors, and took a deep breath.

"This is what really happened," Rick said, as he started typing quickly.

He would scrap his organized crime angle and re-work the story with Goodman, Hoffman, and "Mrs. Lee" as greedy co-conspirators.

Cille was home before long, and Pippa and Charlie fell over themselves jumping off the chair to race down and greet her. Rick followed behind slowly as she called up for him.

"I'm home! Are you still alive?"

"Yes," he said in a slightly questioning tone as he made it down to the kitchen and hugged her tightly. "I was doing some re-writing. The voice I heard in the dream every night was Weinstein's wife. It was her voice saying, 'What was that?' I'm sure of it."

Cille started unpacking the bags and looked skeptical.

"It was me. I yelled it out when I saw your eyes start to flutter open in the hospital. I was so worried, but now I'm so happy."

"How is that possible? That voice and those exact words were the ending of every dream I've had about Ridley since before we met," he insisted.

"Well, my dear," she said kissing him gently on the cheek, "for once you may have been looking into the future rather than backward into the past."

Rick considered that and smiled.

"Maybe you're right. It doesn't matter. I don't care anymore. I'm just glad you're here in my today. The tomorrows will work themselves out."

Chapter 24

Just before Christmas, out on a walk with Pippa and Charlie, Rick pretended he had to tie his boot lace, got down on one knee by the fountain in Washington Square Park, and proposed to Cille. He couldn't decide on the right place or time, but when he thought about how they'd met by chance that Sunday morning at the Allen St. garage, and then again in the park, it seemed appropriate to simply spring it on her when she didn't expect it.

She screamed "Yes!" to the mild applause of a few passersby, and both dogs started barking and jumping when he stood up to kiss her. The dogs did this whenever they hugged or kissed. Usually it was because they wanted undivided attention, but this time it seemed more congratulatory.

When they got home, he noticed Amanda had called right about the time he was proposing, but she hadn't left a message. She was already seven months pregnant, and neither of them had made an effort to stay in touch during the gestation period, so he called her back.

"Well, if it isn't old Gordo," she said jovially.

"Hello! I'm so glad you called. How are you? I have some news, but I want to hear how you and the baby are doing first!"

"I think we both need a vodka. He kicks me from the inside all day and night. He's like a mixed martial artist. This kid needs a cocktail."

"Wait, did you say 'he' kicks you? You're having a boy!"

"Not just a boy, he's my boy, and I'm going to name him Rick."

He assumed it was one of her jokes.

"Yeah, sure. Little Ricky," he said with a laugh.

"Well, if you don't want a namesake I can call him Harry or Peter or something. It's not set in stone."

"You're serious?"

"Of course I'm serious," she said in an offended tone. "When have you known me to kid?"

"Right, I can tell you're not kidding. I'm really flattered. I love you, and I love that little Ricky you've got cooking inside of you."

"So, what's your big news, numbskull?"

"Cille and I just got engaged!"

"That's great! I trust that you're not doing it to yourself again, are you? You know, barking up the wrong tree," Amanda whispered.

"No, this time I've got the right tree," he said laughing. "I can't wait for you guys to meet."

"Let's do it," she said, "but let me get this judo chopper out of my body first. Hey, I also wanted to let you know my cousin Rob is selling that house you liked. The one with the stream!"

"I would love to live there."

"You can," she said flatly. "Just sell your house. You're never there any-way."

"It's funny you say that, because the lease is ending, and they just asked if I'm interested in either extending or selling it to them."

"Well, tell them you're ready. This is your dream home, right? I know we didn't stay long, but you seemed to like it minus the haunting."

"Right, I guess you still don't believe that, but I don't mind."

"Let's just say I'm a skeptic," Amanda drawled.

"Well, it's good to question things," he said with mock encouragement. "Let's talk soon. Let me look into Rob's house. Tell Ricky to simmer down."

"Will do, Gordie. Bye."

Cille was sitting across from him on the couch waiting for an expla-nation after hearing only half of the conversation. They had already talked about making a move, so it seemed reasonable. She owned her apartment, and Rick didn't want to stay in Ian's townhouse much longer even though he had an open invitation. They'd talked about living in her place, but it wasn't really big enough. If they sold both they'd have enough money to buy the house with extra left over in savings. She loved the house based on the listing photos alone and didn't mind moving out of the city since she could do her work remotely, so they called and made an offer the next day.

They set aside a Sunday in late January to go through everything he had stored in the garage and left the dogs in the city so that they could get things done. They had spent the morning going through opened boxes to sort out the important family mementos and salvageable collectibles from the junk and old papers. Even though Rick was prepared to part with anything that wasn't worth moving he felt compelled to analyze every item she pulled from the various bags and boxes. It got easier as the day went on, and it started to feel like a cleansing experience.

Cille went to buy more packing tape, and Rick continued to sort through what he'd consigned to deep storage when the house was rented. He sat down on the bumper of his car and noticed the box in the corner he hadn't opened since Uncle Will died. He bent over and reached in to carefully pull out three smaller boxes, packed them into a fresh box along with the family photos, closed it, and wrote "FAMILY" on the top flap.

It had started to drizzle lightly, and he walked out of the garage and stood looking at the apple tree for a few minutes squinting his eyes through raindrops and tears. He could see himself on the day he and Uncle Will planted it. Standing there, he could smell the soil and the sweat of it; getting the hole deep enough for the size of the root ball and then going a little deeper and wider for good measure with the pickax and spade pulling out rocks and half rotten pieces of old tree root.

Will Gordon was an optimist, so he had gone to a nursery to buy the sapling the day after the funeral as his way of emphasizing that life can triumph even in the face of death. It was just the two of them now. They talked while they dug wiping the sweat and tears on their sleeves, confident they would see the fruit of their labor and that life would prevail. The tree grew year after year but never produced an apple until about 30 years later. Shortly before Uncle Will had gotten the news that he had cancer and wouldn't be getting better the tree put out a profusion of white flowers in May and then started to set fruit. None of them made it to ripeness or full size before being eaten by the squirrels and deer. The tree was sickly, after all. Still, Rick and Will Gordon agreed that this was a sign, finally, that life triumphs over death and also that they didn't waste their time digging the hole that day. His reverie was broken when he saw Cille in his peripheral vision standing in the doorway of the garage holding a large box with her eyes fixed on him.

"I consolidated all of the towels and linens you had in various plastic bags here, and I'm exhausted. I left everything else for you."

"I'm sorry, I didn't even know you were back. I was just thinking about this damn tree. My uncle and I planted it, and I never got one apple out of it."

The rain suddenly came down in thick sheets soaking both of them before they could make it into the garage. They stood there dripping wet and laughing, and she put her head on his shoulder. He had never been happier in his life and started to cry.

"What's wrong, honey? I love you," Cille whispered in his ear.

"I know," he said as he choked back the sudden and unexpected flow of tears. "I love you, too! I'll be OK. I think I'm crying about the stupid tree. I'm sorry."

"It's OK," she said softly. "You have a right. You lived here for most of your life. You and your uncle planted that tree, and it didn't hold up its end of the bargain. It's OK to be sad."

"I know. I'm just afraid it'll start to produce bushels for someone else now that I'm leaving it behind," he said in a serious voice and then smiled as he held her face in his hands. "Besides, we can plant either a real or metaphorical tree at the new house, right?"

"Well, I will always plant one on you," she said softly as she pushed up on her toes and kissed his forehead.

They stood in the garage holding each other tightly as the rain came down harder and flowed in a sheet over the edge of the roof gutter. Her lips and breath were warm on his neck as they embraced, and he never wanted to let her go. He closed his eyes tightly, and it was as if the cold rain outside were sloughing off what was left of his sorrow and loneliness, channeling the remains into small puddles in the gravel driveway before washing it all underground.

Chapter 25

Rick and Cille moved into the house in the middle of March a few weeks after Amanda gave birth to baby Rick. She promised she'd visit as soon as he was at least two months old, and today was the day. They finally felt at home in the old house after distributing their combined furniture and belongings among the small rooms and putting everything else into the carriage barn.

They decided to adopt a dog in the midst of the move. Three just seemed like a good number, and Pippa and Charlie would have a playmate. The dog was four years old and rescued from a puppy mill where they were crossing breeds to make designer hybrids. He was a West Highland terrier who had been used as a sire with odd mates like Pomeranians and Maltese. They weren't producing the best puppies. He was all white, and his fluffy face reminded him of old Ridley's wild, white hair and whiskers, so they named him accordingly. After all, it had been Ridley who brought them together.

For Rick it was also a way of turning Ridley into something positive. He had descended as far as he could go into the depths of the man's life and murder, and he wanted to bring it all back to the surface; away from a subterranean, crypt-like place and into the sunlight. He'd finished editing the manuscript before all of the house activities cropped up but hadn't had a chance to send any queries. He wasn't sure what would come of it, if anything, but he knew he was glad that he wrote it. Cille liked it, and that's the only thing that really mattered.

He was walking around looking for things to childproof in the house and missed a call from Amanda.

"Honey, he isn't old enough to put a fork in the electrical outlet. I think you can relax. This is a little baby," Cille said reassuringly.

"Exactly. This child is defenseless. We can't put him in danger," he said turning to another outlet to install a plastic plug guard.

"Your phone was ringing a few minutes ago. I think you should check and make sure she's coming today before you start installing rubber bumpers on all of the sharp corners."

"Very funny," he said fingering the coffee table suspiciously.

Amanda was already on her way, and he called her back to confirm the directions. The phone rang again just after he hung up, and it wasn't a number he recognized. He answered, and Cille heard a one-sided conversation.

"Yes, hello, who's this? Developing it into what exactly?"

Rick stood with his mouth open for a moment listening.

"You want to make a movie out of my book," Rick said calmly as Cille started jumping around pretending to lasso things around the room.

"Oh, no problem. That's not an issue. I have some material for that," Rick said reassuringly. "Alright, let's talk on Monday. Thanks for calling, Bob."

Rick hung up, and Cille was shifting from foot to foot.

"They're making a film out of your novel?!"

"Not exactly," he said chuckling.

"Then what?"

"He told me the producers think the mobsters should be behind the killings. They said it'll make a better film."

Cille scrunched up her nose. "So what are you going to do?"

"I'm going to give them what they want, of course. I already have an alternate plot. I think they're wrong, but who am I to stand in the way of Hollywood literati or our bank account?"

"How did this happen, honey? You didn't even send it around to anyone yet."

"I can't believe it either! I'd sent the manuscript to Ian, and of course he loved it, since the main character was named after him. I hadn't heard anything else since then, but apparently he knows this guy Bob McMorrow who just called. He works for a production company, and Ian gave it to him without asking me. I would be angry, but you have to admit the guy has the Midas touch!"

Amanda arrived about an hour later with little Ricky Colville in tow. She looked radiant and even healthier than she did in high school as she stepped out of the new SUV that had replaced her convertible.

"Well, this is strange," Amanda said as she pulled the baby from the car seat. "Last time we were here this was my cousin's house, you were alone and unhappy, and I wasn't 'officially' pregnant yet. What a difference a year makes!"

"It was a good year for all of us," he said hugging her from the side and patting the baby on his head.

Amanda and Cille were acting like old friends talking and laughing in the living room while the baby slept in his bassinet. He was worried Amanda would tell Cille some of the less flattering stories from their past, but he knew he couldn't stop her. Cille knew he cleaned up his behavior since he'd met her, so he wasn't too concerned. Pippa, Charlie, and Ridley were curled up in a ball at Amanda's feet, and Cille gently rocked the baby. Everyone was happy.

"I'm going down to the stream to see about catching us some dinner," he said as he put on his jacket.

"Alright," Cille whispered pointing toward the sleeping baby.

"Let's hope you have more luck than last time we were here," Amanda chided.

"We'll see," he said under his breath as he picked up his rubber boots and walked out the door. "Some days you just have to let the fish choose you."

He slid open the carriage barn door to get his rod, net, and lures. As he turned to leave he stopped to look at the box in the corner he'd labeled "FAMILY." He opened the flaps and bent down to carefully lift out the three smaller boxes.

"It's time," he said to himself.

He put on his boots and carried everything down the path to the creek in an old canvas bag that had been hanging on a nail over the fishing gear.

He'd come down to fish the creek a few times since they moved into the house and didn't have a nibble. There had been no sign of John, and Rick was starting to wonder if he could only catch fish when the kindly ghost was nearby. He didn't recall very much from the extended dream state that followed the fall, but he did clearly remember John telling him he needed to go home just before he woke up in the hospital.

He set the canvas bag down on the bank and propped his rod up against a tree. Looking downstream, he glanced up at John's empty house, but there was no smoke coming out of the chimney.

He took the boxes out of the bag and laid them each on a rock. He wasn't sad. He felt calm and resolute. It had been too long. He had held on too long.

Without pausing, he opened each box and poured the ashes into the rushing stream. His mother, father, and uncle were now together, flowing in the water, becoming a part of life again. He'd fulfilled an obligation that had always been too painful to acknowledge, and now it was done.

He picked up his gear and the canvas bag and walked along the shallow side of the creek until he was standing at John's spot. He looked at his small tackle box and pulled out a yellow and black feathered lure with a small silver spinner. Running his finger over the barbless hook and tying it onto his line, he felt as if he'd done this exact same thing before but couldn't remember when. He focused on the swirling pool beyond the log as he cast side-armed toward it and felt a strike as soon as it landed. The fish felt heavy on the line, and it flashed onto the surface as he tried to get an angle to reel it in without getting the line snagged. He carried the net around the side of the log pulling the taught line toward him with his free hand, and the water was nearly over the top of his boots. Then the fish was there, and it was a large rainbow almost as big as the brown he'd caught the first time John pointed out the spot. He wasn't fighting anymore, and the hook slipped out of its mouth as he pulled it into the net. He held it under the flowing water for a moment fingering the knife in his pocket.

"Fish choose you," he could hear John saying, and he quickly cut down-ward from the gills and cleaned it in the water then laid it on a clump of grass on the bank.

Two more large trout took the hook shortly after the first, and he cleaned them and laid them on the grass. He put them into the canvas bag and started making his way back toward the path to the house when he saw smoke rising from John's chimney. He whipped around and looked back toward the spot, but no one was there. He continued walking along the bank and lost his footing on a rock when he heard loud whistling.

Lord preserve us and protect us, we've been drinking whiskey 'fore breakfast…

Rick smiled, looked up toward John's house again, and waved. There was no chimney smoke now, but a blue heron flew overhead flapping its wings slowly as it glided between the trees.

He walked up the muddy path from the creek and started to climb the hill to the house. The dogs had been let out and ran to meet him halfway, and Cille and Amanda followed behind carrying little Rick.

"Well, Gordo," Amanda said happily as he opened the bag to show them the three fish, "you finally fulfilled your manly duties."

"I'm proud of you, honey," Cille said as she kissed him on the cheek.

"Thanks," Rick said hugging them both around the neck, "today was a good day for fishing."